Many Mountains Moving

a
literary
journal
of
diverse
contemporary
voices

seventh issue

Volume III, Number 1

The Day When Mountains Move
Yosano Akiko

———

The day when mountains move has
  come.
Though I say this, nobody believes
  me.
    Mountains sleep only for a little while
That once have been active in flames.
But even if you forgot it,
Just believe, people,
That all the women who slept
    Now awake and move.

This poem was originally published in 1911 in Seitō ("Blue Stocking"), a Japanese literary magazine. It was reprinted from *The Burning Heart: Women Poets of Japan* (translated and edited by Kenneth Rexroth and Ikuko Atsumi, Seabury Press, 1977).

MANY MOUNTAINS MOVING (ISSN# 1080-6474; ISBN #1-886976-06-6) is published three times annually by MANY MOUNTAINS MOVING, Inc., a 501(c)(3) nonprofit organization. First North American Serial Rights. © MANY MOUNTAINS MOVING 1996. Many Mountains Moving, 420 22nd Street, Boulder, CO, 80302, U.S.A. Distributed by International Periodical Distribution. Indexed by the INDEX OF AMERICAN PERIODICAL VERSE (Lanham, MD: Scarecrow Press).

CONTENTS

FICTION

POETRY

ESSAYS

ABOUT THE ARTISTS

ABOUT THE CONTRIBUTORS

Cover Art (pastel on paper), "Tye Bop I," by John Toms

Acknowledgments

We would like to thank the many friends and supporters whose contributions and subscriptions have made this issue possible. We would also like to acknowledge the following people for their help and support: the 1/1 Gallery, AT&T; Tom Auer at *The Bloomsbury Review*; Harriet Boonin; Mark Boscoe, Greg Ramos, and Jonathan Boonin from Arnold & Porter for sharing their legal expertise; Boulder Arts Council; Boulder Bookstore; Mirella Calosci-Sandberg; Mathew Chacko; Lorenzo Chavez; Anita Cheng and Christophe Malbrel; Ramona Chun; Art Coelho; Council and Literary Magazines and Presses for their support with the Gregory Kolovakos Seed Grant; the Denver Women's Press Club; EADS; Yuki and Teruko Horii; International Periodical Distributors; Kinko's; Peggy Lore; Tom and Dale Lowery; Speer Morgan and Greg Michalson at *The Missouri Review*; Reynelda Muse and KCNC-TV 4; Godwin Piyasena and Serendib Printing; Carolyn Takeshita; Tattered Cover; Gene Uba; the Uba family; the Visiones alumni; Chet and Nancy Volpe; and Wild Oats.

Finally, many thanks to our readers, who are dedicated to opening exchange among cultures through art and literature.

"Curious Tyes"
JOHN TOMS
(pastel on paper)

Mood Ring
Karen Auvinen

Melissa does not know what is inside her. She passes through the room of people, invisible, as unseen as a fluttering of breeze or the secret gaze of a lover. She watches people drink and laugh and dance and thinks what a spectacle weddings are. The boat rolls and shifts over the rough water of the lake and Melissa moves toward the long table where her party is seated, aware of the place where her thighs slip past one another as she walks. She sits down and her dress falls open, revealing the strong curve of her calf. She enjoys being on display, though she is certain no one is looking at her.

Before she can say anything, Ed and Judith stand up and move to the aisle between the tables which has become a dance floor. They join the parents of the bride- and groom-to-be and others who jostle and bump against each other, their balance shifting with the roll of the boat and the drinks in their hands. Melissa begins talking to Peter, Judith's husband. Or rather he says something to her, speaking close to her ear, from behind, over her shoulder, because of the band and the sound of the boat. She does not remember what he says exactly, only that for the next two hours, they are talking, their heads bent toward one another.

The journey to the wedding had been just that. Melissa thinks about all those miles by car, the heat of Nebraska and Iowa in late August, crossing the Mississippi River over a great bridge near De Buque, the wide, muddy water like an omen beneath her. Then driving north toward Michigan, through Wisconsin, the land rolling and green, until she knows herself as part of the landscape, moving her hand along her side, down over her hip, the fleshy curve of her belly. Her skin is hot and sticky as the air, nettled with a fever she does not know she has. On her finger is a mood ring shaped like an open flower, like the one she had when she was just a girl. It is cheap and made of bendable metal so that she can make it fit any finger on her hand and she wears it because it reminds her of the girl she was and the woman she has become. The center is black now because she is so hot. It looks like some surreal flower on her finger with its black center and silver petals.

Melissa likes to travel by car, the movement of one rise to the next, covering all those miles in one long caress. The days pass outside of time, the way they do when one is on the road, full of landscape slipping beneath the eye along with the vague feeling that out here anything is possible. Melissa feels as if she is in a dream, not necessarily her own. When she comes to, it is too late, but that is later, after she has arrived at the pre-wedding festivities, after she is already on the boat talking with Peter, after she has excused herself from the party and disappeared into the dark shadow of midnight air.

The first night, they stop in Madison to stay with friends of Peter and Judith. Melissa does not know any of these people, except for Ed whom she met in college and they treat each other with the kind of distance common among people of different ages. She is the youngest of this group by at least twenty years, and it settles the feeling of distance and time that has characterized this journey. She does not view her companions as old, nor herself as young, though she feels the difference between them, keeps telling herself, *This is not me, I am not like that.*

Melissa excuses herself as Peter and Judith and Ed sit down with their hosts for daiquiris. She walks down to the lake in the center of town, gazing out over the smooth body of water and the setting sun, trying to hold it, trying to hold something, inside her. She tries to meditate there by the lake, hoping to empty her body of this feeling of scraping up against things, the fine raw edges of her flayed by the wind, but she feels oddly unsettled, somehow out of place. Nothing seems to stick. She is a swimmer in a vague ocean; there is something just beneath her belly, she can feel it in the dark recess of the water which pulls at her. Her closed eyelids flutter; she is distracted by the wind, the feeling of difference and worry that someone might speak to the woman who is sitting silently by the lake.

Melissa stays until she worries her absence might somehow be impolite and she returns to the house where the circle of friends is sitting and laughing over their drinks. Later that night, after dinner, after they have gone on a walk in the neighborhood to the church where Larry is a pastor, after they have settled in for cookies and coffee in the living room, after Peter has excused himself to go shower, after they are talking, Melissa is thinking of the trip and wondering what the passage of this land has meant. Her gaze is on the floor near her feet when she senses Peter entering the room. She raises her head slowly, not necessarily deliberately, though she knows later this is the effect. Peter is standing in the hallway watching her, or rather, she thinks, watching his effect on her as she lifts her eyes from the floor, traveling the inevitable distance of his body which is the potent body of someone who shapes his environment to suit himself. At fifty-nine, Peter is stronger than most men Melissa knows, his torso and arms thick and capable. Suddenly, he seems to her like the only solid thing in the room. Her eyes come to rest on his face, which is wide and strong, like a river she wants to cross. She is unearthed; there is a moment of recognition and then it is gone. Some time passes before Melissa realizes she has stopped moving, that she is sitting perfectly still, that Peter has stopped too, the sarong-like garment he wears knotted in a twist in the space between his navel and his groin, his T-shirt, tight and wet from his hair, which is a fine grey-black, hanging past his shoulders, hanging in thin, wet strips down his back. His blue eyes are on her, watching what she will do. Suddenly, the conversation returns, a rush of noise in an empty room. Mary is saying *And what about Bosnia...?* and they all mumble and whisper, *terrible...terrible....*

Peter is talking, bent toward her. They are at dinner now and Melissa is seated at the head of the table between Peter and Ed. They drink wine, sending the attendant back again and again for *just one more bottle* as guests take turns toasting the groom-to-be.

Melissa and Peter have continued their conversation from earlier and when she thinks back to it now, she does not remember what he says, cannot think of more than half a dozen phrases and glances. It does not matter though. The sound of his voice, his eyes watching her watch him. She knows she could talk to him all night. It all seems too easy, how well they fit each other. Melissa can see inside him; they have the circuits, the same explosive wiring.

She thinks herself out of time to have met this man, old enough to be her father, not her father. Staring at him, lips moving, hands so close to hers, she imagines what they would feel like on her body, imagines him slipping one up the length of her exposed leg right there, right now. She wants his mouth on her, between her legs, wants him to say *I want to fuck you, I want to fuck you* over and over.

Melissa takes a sip of her wine and turns as the father of the bride begins to make a speech. She can feel Peter looking at her, her legs exposed beneath the dress, the side of her face turned from him, the place where her bra hints at the breast beneath. She wants him to watch her, wants him to guess what she is thinking over her smile, the glass of wine held loosely in her hand.

This color must mean you need another drink, Peter says, pointing to her ring. Melissa looks down at her finger to the place where Peter is touching her with the tip of his. The color is light blue: her hands must be cold. Then she notices the missing petal, one small arc of silver detached in the night, lost in the journey from there to here. *I don't know,* she says, *I don't know what it means.*

From the deck, Melissa can see nothing but water. The waves hiss and roll against the boat, and the night and low clouds obliterate the world. Earlier, she had stared into the eyes of a married man and for the first time in her life, she has wanted something no matter what. She fears her passion, the conviction of her ragged desire. Angered that what she wants is not hers for the taking, she staggers under the bare electricity and coarse nerves circuiting her body. She begins to pull at the petals of the ring, bending them one by one until they break. She lets them fall between her fingers like so many pieces of bread marking the trail.

Melissa is suspended in space; she wills herself to touch something solid: the white painted railing, the jacket of the man standing next to her.

"Hi," she says, looking up into the night, her hand pressing down his arm for support.

"You're one of the writers, like Jim," he says, smiling, not seeming to mind her hand or the tilt of the boat which throws them together.

"Yes, we went to college together."

"In Boulder? I've never been to Colorado...." And so it begins, she thinks, as the man, whose name is Harold and who is here because he knows someone whose name she cannot remember and who has luscious black curly hair and strong hands and who is exactly her age, leans toward her, speaking close to her face, his words fueled by the courage of too much to drink and the womb of the boat over the dark lake.

And soon she is leaning against him, leaning into him, trying to find solid ground on this boat which continues to rock and sway as the band plays beneath their feet, the floor of the deck vibrating with the pulse of music.

"Let's get out of the wind," she says and the two move back to the stern, out of the wind and the rain, for now it has begun to rain. They stand next to stairway housing, facing out to whatever they have left behind. A woman bends over the railing, vomiting from the mixture of whitefish, alcohol, and the waves.

No one sees them. The man stands behind her, his hands moving over her breasts, into her dress, down her sides. Melissa can feel him shaking and she is reminded of times she made out in cars when she was younger, the awkwardness of it, the same seedy feel of the forbidden. She lets the sway of the man's body carry her; she is submerged, unwilling to resist, wanting to be pulled down, to forget, *to forget*. He kisses her sloppily—the wet, beer-laced kisses of someone who is lonely and desperate.

There, in the shadow of the boat, she puts her hands behind her, feeling for his hardness, reaching for a commonness between them. She rubs up the front of his pants, slipping her hand into the waistband, beneath the belt and then unbuckling the belt and loosening the pants. She pulls him toward her. As she does this, the man removes his overcoat and pulls it over the front of her, draping them in their own corner of night.

Suddenly, he pushes himself against her and there is that instant ache in her, that delicious feel of emptiness, the moment of craving before satisfaction. Hauling her dress up, he gathers it into his fist at her side, driven now by something that has nothing to do with her. He pulls her closer, positioning himself between her legs, then into her from behind, pressing himself into her soft spot, which opens and opens. The man whispers into her ear, talking to himself as much as to her, telling her *yes* and *I want you* and *I want to come*.

For Melissa, there is only this: the sound of him breathing in her ear, the feel of him inside her and the crush of the material beneath her fingers. The rain, the night, the tilt of the boat, everything that has happened until now, until this very moment, leave her. They are cast from her like leaves in the wind and she lets them go, unable to hold them any longer. It is then that she realizes how big the world is, how immense the movement of things and it makes her feel very small, clinging to her anonymous lover on the edge of the boat sailing out of and into nowhere. *I want to come,* he says, and knowing he will not last much longer, she presses her hand between her legs to speed her own release. And when she finally comes, she begins to cry not because of what she has done, but because the ground is moving again and the world comes spinning back.

Later, the next day, after the wedding, after everything as Melissa stands on the veranda of the hotel, she will look out over the bay and remember the ring, which she dropped like some desperate anchor into the water on the dark night before.

"Big Daddy Jazz"
JOHN TOMS
(pastel on paper)

Sea Song
Alison Stone

Each night she lies patiently in fire,
Blood thick, body dissolving.
Dissatisfaction is religion.
She plants it and prays. She cuts
His meat and licks blood from the knife.

Some nights he stumbles
Into her grief, which tries
To drown him like an invisible well.
He is a wolf with no teeth,
He is a blind soldier
Shooting everything, he is
An ear of corn beneath the beaks of crows.
If only sorrow had shape
He could climb it like rope
To the attic where their marriage waits.

Husband and wife
—they touch, recede.
They sleep.

And It Was Morning, It Was Evening
Alison Stone

Loving is a room I enter sideways
Dragging my stump.
Our bodies burn like trees.
Roots of gut, branches of bone.

Our faces have left us.
Whatever ties us to our lives has vanished
Screeching in the owl's beak.
Wet and boneless, we are maggots feeding
Beneath the rock of the dark.
Our mouths open to hold coral and stars.

Stillborn
Alison Stone

for Jody & Pat

Look my husband
What our love has made.
Lying in my arms
He is peaceful and perfect.
He has all his limbs and scraps
Of moss-like hair,
Exactly ten fingernails.
He does not wet or cry.

Eight months I swelled with him,
I grew beyond myself.
You pressed your ear
Against my belly hearing hiccups,
Felt the kicks that made me smile.

God ignores me
When I cry for Him,
Will not tell me why a heart beats,
A particular heart,
Chosen somehow to fuel a body
And to stop.

Before the stillness grew to where
It could not be ignored
And the doctors with their drugs
Forced me to spit him out,
I thought I was a fertile field.
Unaware, I glided through the days with joy,
But my body was the grave of our son.

The Book
Alison Stone

Nothing needs to be touched
Except bodies.
When the child lies crying
In the mother's arms,
When the father smooths
The satin of her face,
The book of her life
Begins to write itself
In a language beautiful and true.

Nothing needs to be touched
Except bodies.
When the body of the boy
Is cut by his father's belt,
When the body of the girl
Is opened,
When the river of the brother's pain
Or the sister's pain
Flows to the ear of the child,
Then disease is scrawled upon the pages
Of the body's book.

The man can read the child's story
In the woman's flesh.
His fingers scan boustrophedonic chapters
While his body mimics love.
What is hurt and weak in her calls out
To what is hurt and cruel in him.
They are locked together
Like a corpse and its shadow.

Deep beneath the skin
Where spirit joins the bones,
Lies the pool that is the many lifetimes
Of the woman or the man.
Injuries and crimes float,
Bloated, dank,

While the book
Of the true and beautiful is drowned.

The rare woman or man
Who is both lucky and brave
Will dive into the lake
To shine a candle on the hidden wounds
And speak their truth
Until the body lets go
Of the story of the parents.
Then the book of life, though worn
And shorter than the child's book,
Holds beneath its covers
Pages that remain to be written.

Myrmidons
Patrick Pritchett

O, my evening,
my breadbasket,
my muddy garden so
grateful for the rain,

how do you do
what you do
to make me feel
there's a lamp inside my hand,

that nothing special
is everything,
like the air,
or a Mahler adagio?

It's like a movie
where one guy
makes a crack
to another

that's rude
and tender and funny,
or the woman laughs
at the hero's

discomfiture
and we know
right then how
much she loves him.

It's sad, too,
like our dads coming home
late from work,
like Achilles coming

back to the tent
after a long day of it.
It's before the quarrel
with the King started;

he slaps Patroclus
on the back,
jesting to cover
heart and bone-ache,

and props the great spear,
wet with blood,
in the corner,
where it shines, stern and black,

lit by a few faltering candles.
The sea sounds close by—
the murmur of oinopa ponton,
wine poured into darkness.

Outside, the firefly
names of the Myrmidons
pray to Artemis
of the scabbard moon

because tonight
she is most beautiful
and in the grass tomorrow
Death will shave their long hair

in ceremonial curls.
O Prince, whose
ankle is a flower,
the iron that bent

your heart forever
is melting inside
this rain, which whispers
this evening

unsung Iliads
by the garden,
whispers to anyone
who will stop to listen

the secret names
of the Myrmidons,
who fell with
the sweet rose of breath

still blooming
inside their wrists and ankles.
Loyal to the earth in their falling.
Grateful for the rain, as I am.

Magpiety
Patrick Pritchett

The way stones are a part of earth,
and don't ever seem to want to leave it,
is the way the magpie
alights
in the topmost branch of the ash,
and sways a moment, rocking
back and forth, tail augering
the air for support,
the complications
of so much mass confounded
by the miracle of such lightness.
Matter: what liquefies
in our hands.
"All things are made of water," Thales said.
This piece of Precambrian gneiss on my desk
still flows in the stillness of its metamorphosed river.
And air that beats and holds the magpie aloft
is the same air that will not let us drop.

Even the Stones Have Names
Ingrid Wendt

Here is where we live, I'm pointing (Harald
translating). Mountains, here where it's green,
east and west of our city, no more than an hour's
drive to go skiing, or to the beach, and Eugene
has just about everything: opera, ballet, health
foods, tofu (all week I've been planning this scene),

and here is Tucson. My mother lives in Tucson.
Here in Arizona. (I've brought the map with me,
pictured this route to sharing our lives, in Finnmark;
something to offer Harald's mother, Kristine.)
Three days by car, to Tucson, it's that far away.
But she was born in Michigan. That's even

farther. My sister's in upstate New York.
And here is Illinois, the place I'd dream of,
if I dreamed of home. I grew up in town,
and Ralph, on an Iowa farm his sister's keeping
going. Our daughter's in Italy, working.
She's fine. We try not to worry. This scene,

just as I envisioned, back home in Eugene.
But something else has been added—our week with Harald
and Britt, with Kristine—and without warning, between us,
invisible, swaggering, there for all of us
to see, that old assumption: it's natural, leaving
behind our family, our home. Yesterday Harald took us

past the birches he used to get lost in—between
his mother's house, where he was born, and the house
his father's brother built (now his own)—green
leaves deeper than green, full of midnight
sun, and a tangle of flowers I'd never dreamed
survived here—took us down to the river to fish.

Past the place the German army, retreating,
burned the turf hut where his mother was born.
Past the salmon nets—all those centuries leaning

into the current, rows of wooden poles
bedded in Sami tradition—and past the creeks
whose mouths on the Tana have always offered fish

whose names Harald told us, and told us, *here
in Tana, even the stones have names*. Yesterday,
the sun on our backs, with Harald and Aslak and Siri,
the sun off-center, each moment was full of forever.
This map was a way I thought we'd meet each other.
This map is a stone in my heart.

Questions of Grace
Ingrid Wendt

1.

Somehow, it's cows we've decided are stupid.
And pigs. Chickens, too, therefore all
the more edible, though we deplore the conditions
they sometimes are raised in, egg to hatchet

cramped on the assembly line, never scratching
gravel as they were born to do, or cocking a voice
to the sun. Some of my friends, of course, will eat
only that which is brainless, which never had

even the slightest song of its own. To whom
but the Norwegians can I confess not only have
I eaten reindeer stew, salami, blood balls, but
last night, here in Norway, I ate Vågehval, Lesser

Rorqual, *Balaenoptera Acutorostrata*, yes, last night
I ate a steak of whale, tender and
thick as filet mignon. It was good.

2.

Ánde Somby, Sami lawyer, son
of reindeer herders descended from
reindeer herders farther back than anyone
knows, tells how when his father had to kill
one of his own he talked to it, petted it, "Deer,
I'm sorry you happened to be here just at this
wrong time. Whose fault is it I do this?"

Here in Samiland, all is used. I've seen
the way the skin of the skull is stretched
on birch-twig frames just the right size for boots;
and sinew turns into thread; antlers, to buckles;
bones, to straws to filter drinking water.
I think of the Coos, the Takelma, the Kalapuya back home.

It was much the same way. Back home, those people are gone.

3.

Last week at the Tromsø museum, I learned two
or three coastal villages still are allowed to
hunt for whale, and in each village, five
to ten boats, and in each boat, a five-

to ten-whale limit, May through July, adults
only; and always some government person's on board,
testing the meat, doing some research, counting.
Twenty thousand left in these waters, no fear

of extinction. I learned the whalers, following still
the steps of their parents, their parents' parents before them
(once feeding not only their children but also the life
blood of Norway) would certainly profit more today, fishing cod.

4.

Years, now, and my mother
each time we visit, wrestles
the question of grace.

>   *God is great, God is good,*
>   *and we thank him for our food.*

That's ok, she says, but
>   *By His goodness we are fed,*
>   *give us, Lord, our daily bread,*

why ask for what we've already got?

You're right, we tell her.
We say the grace again.
We eat.

5.

Back home, our neighbors, the few
Sundays we ate there, they
made up something new each time.

We heard the grievous errors of our ways.
We heard again the sin of our ingratitude.
We heard the names of all those needing blessing,

including ourselves. Heavenly Father, the food

always got cold.

6.

Late afternoon and the Tromsø sky again
has drifted shut, a solid white porcelain bowl, hill
to hill, except for one small overlay, one
single stretch of silver, long as a squid, the shiny lure

Siri (eleven) cast again and again last week in the Tana River,
Harald rowing against the current almost an hour
to keep us in place, the reeds along the bank
promising *strike*, the pools where grayling for decades

used to hide and in past years have disappeared and then
the reeling it in, such happiness, six inches long,
the skinny dumb fish she picked up and kissed and kissed and
later, for supper, ate.

7.

And still, I've found a restaurant here in town with
dishes I can't bring myself to eat: bear bouillon
(with rye bread and butter); barbequed bear ribs; grilled
bear fillet; Siberian bear meat casserole. Is it
just personal?

                        For the Sami, the bear is a sacred
animal; hunting it, eating it, everyone knows the rules.
What would they think if they knew that I myself once
talked with a bear in the wilds, persuaded that bear
to leave me alone?

And what if I'd talked with a whale?

8.

By what sign in the market
do we know the spirit?

By what rituals
are we permitted to eat it?

9.

Reader, somewhere in the coast range
of Oregon, have you heard about this? Some

physicist somehow wired a grove of trees for sound.

When one
tree was cut down, it emitted a cry.
When that tree cried, the rest of the grove cried, too.

10.

Green things: spinach, peas, cabbage, kale,
zucchini, pole beans, broccoli, dill, how to
measure the songs of that chorus of chlorophyll?

11.

And who is to say the rocks are not
also alive? And the hills?
Last week I walked over tundra.
What from the car seemed barren, forlorn,
was totally covered with mosses, lichen, every
color of sunset, horizon
to horizon.
        And at the coast, at home,
trying to gather mussels, go fishing,
the stones we clamber over, what barnacles just
starting out do we crush? What larvae
of starfish, silent as galaxies, just
that far from our own recognition?

Last week a poet showed me a stone,
the size of a football, smoother than skin.
Hold it, he said, with care.
Between your hands, it will breathe.

12.

Reader, what
day do we not trade
at least one voice for our own?

Where,
and with what words
do we dare place our feet?

Elusive Powers
Lowry Pei

"A thought comes when 'it' will, not when 'I' will...the subject
. 'I' does not condition the predicate 'think.'"
—Nietzsche, *Beyond Good and Evil*

Much has been written, and probably always will be, about writing as if it were something under the writer's guidance. My purpose here, by contrast, is to walk reflectively around the outskirts of the creative faculty, knowing that it is outside myself, other than myself, and its working is impossible to describe. I've been writing fiction and non-fiction, some of it published, for twenty years, and teaching writing for longer than that—being in the neighborhood while the creative power, on its own schedule, got some work done for me and others. It seems to me that after this long I can begin trying to say what it's like to work in some sort of collaboration with that which I do not control.

For me, the experience of writing a first draft involves a lot of waiting, for a voice in the head that comes, as Nietzsche says, when *it* will, not when *I* will, from an unidentified source. While I wait, my job is to try to keep my attention focused on the subject at hand—not to think up sentences, not to string words together like the plastic beads that plug into each other to form a child's necklace. Doing that would be pointless, distracting; what I have to do is wait and try to keep my attention on the problem, the scene, the train of thought. Eventually the voice says something relevant—maybe only a phrase. Perhaps I begin writing at once, or perhaps I wait for a sentence to form itself. Perhaps I repeat those first words with my conscious mind, listening to how they sound, wondering if they could sound better, if they make sense. Perhaps I try to deduce logically where the sentence is going; already, even before the sentence is formed, I'm doing something like revising. The sentence does not get finished, usually, by such deduction, but that deductive activity seems to help trigger the voice that is the source, and what the voice eventually says is usually different from, and truer than, what I had managed to deduce. Sometimes the voice gets freed up and carries me along for several sentences or even, when I'm lucky, a whole paragraph at a time; often it doesn't and I spend a great deal of my writing time waiting, re-reading, tinkering, correcting, doing anything I can to keep my mind somewhere in the vicinity of my subject, until the voice says the next thing that I will write down.

The voice that writes is often very faint, and goes by very quickly. I find that I have to be very good at eliminating distractions, including those that come from within, and fast in recording what the voice says. It sometimes seems barely to surface into consciousness, as if a banner fluttered for a moment above the surface of a choppy lake, just long enough for me to glimpse an inscription on it, then disappeared beneath the waves. In a few seconds it will be forgotten; even the fact that something surfaced will be forgotten; it will be as if nothing ever happened, unless in those few seconds I write down what I glimpsed there. The voice that speaks what's worth writing down is sometimes one among a crowd of voices, and far from the loudest. It speaks in the interstices left by the other voices chancing to shut up; although it may be that chance has nothing to do with this, it seems that way. There is no accompanying announcement that this is the thing I'm supposed to pay attention to; in fact, other voices, talking about something like what to cook for dinner, are generally announcing themselves as if over a public-address system, in a tone which suggests that their agenda must be considered at once. Part of learning to write, for me, has been learning where the attention needs to go, and how to help it stay on the alert for the small voice that matters, but that does not preface what it says with "I am the voice that matters."

Of course there are those moments when the voice that does the writing is absolutely self-assured, when it takes full possession of the mind to the exclusion of all else. Those moments are transcendent or ecstatic, and the hope of repeating them is probably what makes me want to write. But they're rare, and I can't depend on such moments to get my writing done—the moments when the voice is so strong that instead of listening for it I become it; I have had to learn to give my attention deliberately the rest of the time, in a very specific way.

For me writing has a great deal to do with meditation—letting go of distracting thoughts without allowing the letting go to become an effort that in itself constitutes a distraction. A practice of ceasing to try and starting to allow. There is impatience to be transcended, and also fear—the fear of sitting quietly without distractions. What if I should find nothing within myself? What if I should find something?

The search as I experience it is definitely for something that is already there inside. What I need to know, I believe, is always in front of my nose, like the purloined letter, and almost perfectly hidden there—but the key word is "almost"; the obvious, long contemplated, yields the most sought-after revelations. The object of the game is not to search for some esoteric part of myself, a sort of Northwest Passage of the soul; the object is to stay home and sink down into the reality of home—the soul's home—to sink down into the exact reality of the self, the reality that I most deeply long to explore or become. What I've learned through writing and teaching seems to be that the mistake is not to go deep enough. At a superficial level we can talk and be sure of what everyone means (though not much can be said); at a middle level, each soul is separate from each other and we despair of communication; at a deep level, where art lives, by diving into the center of the self, we reach others where they want to be reached. Our most private, most personal intuitions and longings, the ones we fear are incommunicable and the ones we are generally trained to hide, seem strangely enough to be the very basis of communication.

But wait: didn't I contradict myself by suggesting that the voice came from outside of me and then saying that I have to sink deeply into myself? Maybe not, if I go on to say that the inmost self is collective, or that sinking in is a way of opening to the transcendent...however these two aspects of the experience are to be reconciled, they are both the case. Within versus without is a false distinction.

When I revise in the sense of rewriting sentences—when I stand off as the reader and look at the work from an artificial distance—I operate on the words more consciously, and more controllingly, than not. As I read I monitor how I am making the sentences mean something, and what I am making them mean—what I would make them mean if I had to start from the words on the page rather than from the impulse that drives me to write. If I catch the reader-part of me making the words mean something that the writer-part doesn't want to mean, I try to change the words on the page so that they will operate upon that reader-part of my mind in the way that the writer-part intends. All of this sounds something like playing all four hands in a game of bridge—complex, but calculable in an analytical way. Nevertheless, there are many points in a revision where simply weighing word choices isn't enough—where whole new sentences must come into being—and there the unconscious, or uncontrolled, faculty comes into play again.

But that's only the linguistic level of revision; that level assumes that I know what I want to mean, which is far from always being the case. This discussion is also misleading if it leaves out the fact that any new sentence I write down may very well change what I mean; the meaning I am intending is not a fixed quantity—language changes it. Writing is not a one-way action of intention upon language; simultaneously, language acts upon intention. For this reason, revision can go on forever—language altering intention, altered intention changing language, and so on, chasing a meaning that is always disappearing around the corner. Usually the only way to end this chase is to search back instead of searching ahead, to return to my first impulse, the first intimation that drove the piece of writing into existence, and to think my first thought again—not think about it, but actually think it. Inwardly live it again. Start over again the creation of the world which is this piece of writing. Then words may come as if for the first time.

Any piece of writing worth prolonged work is alive; it is trying to be something. Even if I don't know what that something is, I can feel the piece trying to emerge from itself. To finish a piece I must at some time jump to—I was going to say an understanding, but I really mean an inhabitation of what the piece is trying to be, and work from that; that jump is an instinctive leap in the dark. Even if it is, as I have suggested, a jump back to what I always knew about the piece, my own knowledge comes as a kind of surprise, and the creative power cannot be pushed to make the leap; it will do so in its own good time.

Because I must somehow inhabit the world of the piece of writing before that world even exists, before I know what words I will use to speak it, thus live in it and know it before it has attributes to be inhabited and known—because this logically impossible feat is absolutely essential to writing as I experience it, I can never sum writing up as a superior form of craftwork, cabinet-making to the *n*th degree. No matter how much technique I have, or may come to have—and I feel the need for a great deal of it—all exercise of craft is secondary to an action that I always perform without knowing how.

There are plenty of things about writing fiction that I can do on purpose, such as avoiding weak repetitions or unintentional rhymes, but the important things must initiate themselves; in fact, to the extent that I am bringing scenes, characters, or events into existence by an act of will, they come out lame and untrue. Telling the creative faculty what to create does not work. And if it's true that I don't tell myself what to create, still less can it be true that I knowingly create what conventional wisdom tells me to. Society may or may not condition my unconscious, but that's a different issue. Even if it turns out that I create to order, I am not aware, and must not be aware, of following orders while the creative process is unfolding. It's not so much a case of trying to be original as that at least the sensation of originality is necessary in order for anything to be created. For me, the elusiveness of the creative process lies partly in this: the imagination, when doing its essential work, notices the other—that which it is not directed to notice. Exactly there, in that realm of the other, the not-commanded noticing, lies a margin of play, a "vacant paradise" in the words of a poem by James Wright.

This margin of play seems to be threatened with diminution as our species more and more thoroughly dominates and domesticates the planet and our own selves, takes control of the physical and spiritual environment in which we live. As we try to create the conditions in which our humanity can flourish—free ourselves from never-ending obsession with survival—we also threaten that humanity by making more and more of the world into a commanded reality, an already-defined reality in which each element, drained of mystery, more and more becomes what it is said to be and no more. A world in which Coke is the real thing. But we are constantly rescued by the elusive nature of thinking and creativity, by the way this faculty always manages to make its escape; it refuses to be defined, it remains outside the controlled world, and because it does that, it persists in finding the otherness which is concealed right out in the open all around us. Somehow, imagination lives in an original world (a world of origin, of coming-into-being) in which the self meets a reality that is what it unspeakably is, too powerful to be summed up in any formula of words no matter how complex. This encounter in an original world can take many forms: physical adventure, spiritual discipline, the making of art works, romantic love, scientific investigation….I won't pretend to complete the list. But wherever a particular temperament finds it, it is always a risky encounter that is its own reward, a lonely encounter in one sense because one enters it as oneself with nothing to fall back on, and the reverse of lonely because in it—finally!—one meets a presence which asks for, and accepts, everything one can give.

There is a traditional story of a man who loses a quarter one evening in his back yard: later his wife finds him looking for it under the street lamp in front of their house.

"Why are you looking for it out there?" she asks him.

"Because the light is better here," he replies.

Perhaps language is the street lamp; perhaps consciousness itself. In any case, the quarter remains in the back yard, undisturbed by any investigations out front—an inexhaustible source of wealth.

The Trail to Avalanche Lake
Dina Coe

When he says, Rocks are new potatoes,
his lover, me, sees Red Bliss
in all its sizes, scrubbed by rain.
Cushioned on cedar chips and breathing cedar sweat,
we're encompassed by another world:
a rainforest beneath the glacier peaks.
And rain plus red potato flour
makes pudding. That's the milky Avalanche
gumming up our soles as we climb the unknown
distance to the lake. However long it takes,
we're stuck in it, me ahead, or him
working redbrown, light-boned limbs,
sending back a racy whiff.
When he turns, his smile embraces
whatever he sees in me. Round the bend,
gathering as it cascades, a creek
froths crystals like a rocky head
on the mountain's ice-blue drink.
This is no soft brew touted by an ad,
but the real ideal of freshness, so other
than we're used to, we shouldn't drink it
without boiling first. What gives the tint
(a ranger said) is glacial flour.
That's rock dust ground by glaciers.
She said that wildflowers too eat granite,
making bare cliff digestible for tree roots.
The earth is food.

Bathing in Kachina Hot Springs
Pamela Uschuk

for Maria Teresa Acevedo

I

We unmoor from our bodies,
anemones healing in the thermal stream,
faces tilted like sunflowers
toward the bloody hieroglyph of sun
inscribed behind our closed lids.
Each muscle seized is undone
at the sacred feet of Mt. Graham
while Geronimo spins,
come back as a dust devil,
his broad shoulders a dervish of gold sand
as he dances down deer to browse.
Time breathes from their mouths.

Otter woman, water bearer, you bask
in healing steam, dream
clay half-fills your ancestral home
in Aravaipa Canyon, where
your grandfathers farmed deltas
and the dark slopes of night for stars,
where moon-eyed as coyotes
they hunted jack rabbits, deer
and big-horn sheep along
the limber song of the creek they adored.
At the millenium's breach, your family
can't recall their Opata tongues.

You dream your canyon crumbles
like dry tortillas, half-fills with clay
and you lie mummified,
relic of love and questions
returned to the hands of sandstone
and wind who spun your shape
while I converse with deer who gather
information in a high meadow, circling.

Sing, your charge is to sing,
the deer urge in blue wind voices.
Get the story right.
Learn the vast seasons of humility
flattening desert, the apocalyptic storms
that save everything.
Ocean becomes desert
and earth becomes the wind.
Even earth can tire of spring.
Sing, the deer whisper deep as grass,
deep as turquoise veining canyon walls.

II

I think of Geronimo, how
he defied decades of soldiers
in these mountains deciphering
each direction of wind, how
he turned up like a dinner invitation
from a lost friend, knocking
on the red door of the rental car,
how he led us to these pools to dream
after we drove your disabled mother
to her trailer and fed her tortillas,
chicken and the seven steroids
the doctor prescribed for crippling arthritis,
your mother who all her life cleaned
the houses of the rich and infirm.

I tell you that my mother,
whose body is limber, who tends
my invalid father she's loved
half a century, now goes blind.
Nurses binding the world's wounds,
where is justice and
what is our true legacy?
What can we defy?

Drifting in steaming blue, my body
half keels, rights itself, a lost raft,
buoy of time and fortune, and I see
a hawk split the sky we breathe,
split the deer's blue song,

my heart's four-chambered melody
naked in my naked chest,
a hawk diving with its death shriek
clutched in the killing beak.
How many ways there are
                            to die, then
the sudden upswing to survive.

Women precipiced at midlife, we wonder
which choices bring down the stars,
which turn to lead slugs that clog the machine.
Childless women, we are armed
against loneliness with the certainty
of the deer's obsidian climb
up hardscrabble cliffs
scored by the hawk's quick screech.
Childless women, we are armed
with weaponry stamped love.

> My friend, we come home.
> Home now to the liquid arms
> sweetening the center of rock old as time. We have
> arrived.

III

You and I are bright as mica, afloat
in memory's long aquamarine pool,
our thighs brushing, breasts
and stomachs refashioned
by the mineral hands of water
from the mountain that intersects sky.
We fall into constellations our grandmothers
named gods for our sakes.

> Blue mountain,
> sacred mountain, bloodied
> by dawn, by dusk's stigmata,
> mountain astonished by a flurry of wings
> outlasting all questioning.
> Holy mountain bulldozed
> for government contracts,
> for the telescope
> extending astronomers' eyes.

Do you hear your grandmother
calm as Aravaipa cliffs, see her
unlined hands squeeze clay
to shape pots into the heads of deer,
the sweet piping of canyon wrens
who divine rock for light?

I hear my grandmother warn me
as she weaves a mat of strawberry grass
and dandelion greens. Love,
love hard, love wide
as the sunbent heart of wind
that defines everything.
Keep your eye to the horizon
beyond betrayal,
beyond greed,
                my grandmother sings,
velvet moth relieved of her husbands' deceits,
velvet moth green and bright as the moon.

I turn my face in the water
and your dark hair angels your profile
carved from the mask of Mayan Jaguar kings.
I remember how the pyramids terrified your soul,
how in a rainforest where the quetzel flies,
you found your own obsidian head
buried deep in earth.

Oh, sweet sister, to sweat like this
in the torrid afternoon sheets of late summer,
neck deep in a thermal sea
miraculous in a desert thirsty as its name.

Oh, to leak all sorrow,
all grief of the might have been
children, the rainless seasons of our wombs.

We sleep in the numinous hands of water
piped from the lucid hearts
of granite mountains duplicating themselves
like giant star clusters, laughing
in their shifting coats of blue mist
above the spin of Geronimo,
above the porcelain clatter of deer hooves

tapping out syllabics of desire between arid thorns,
above the hawk digesting her kill,
above the near coil of the rattler
loving us, loving us.

IV

Now it is migration time,
the thick afternoon before the harvest moon.
Outside the cotton is waist deep,
slick green leaves,
hives of pesticides
insulting the ancient peaks.
Is it any wonder Geromino spins
drilling anger to the four winds,
that hawk bones thin, eggshells
crack, arthritis cribs
joints shattering of their own weight.

Who can breathe tonight?

Your mother says so many people
get cancer here in this valley,
even couples die sixty days apart.
The spray is like gauze in her face.
Cotton growers complain they're going broke
but who holds all those coins?

V

How far can we dream
to retrieve our buried hearts?

I touch your hand
soft as velvet dust on a moth's wing
that glides each lick of tide
moving the shore of this old sea we navigate.

Dear friend, when you die
into another life, who will kiss
your wrists alive?

We enter the sacred waters,
the water enters us
until we evaporate into wind

that scales the pitched octaves of treeless peaks,
witnessing everything,
unmoved, undestroyed symphony
radiant with gravity, with passing light.

VI

Geronimo bends to stroke away the lines
dividing our sight, to
still lightning that would slice
dreams from the mundane.
He is our witness
as much as that hawk,
cocking his vain head,
his yellow eye entering ours
to celebrate the eternal pitch
of his cry—
the mnemotic shapes of hunter and prey
and the lines that blur
changing everything.

What can we know
except those we love
and the stories brambling our lives?

In the arroyo throb
strobed between my eyes, we dance
spinning naked as lotuses, our tongues
untied as our grandmothers'
ululating the clear syntax of stars,
metaphors of hope and wind
against sorrow, against the greed of men.

You lie still as an altar
in blue water, the brown clay of your skin
kneaded by your grandmother's fingers,
while your mother's arthritic clasp
is restored sweet and lithe
as the first music calling
the cells of the hawk to fly.

No Man's Land
Michael Dorsey

My brother and I have had this same dream before. I think it is one we all have in one form or another: he is running, or it might be you, and you are coming through the corn. The world is green on all sides except for the path underfoot, which is brown and soft. Your feet sink with every footfall; the ground is betraying you. You're running as fast as you can despite a side stitch and if you can only make it to the old fallen log at the edge of the field you know you'll be safe. It is a boundary our pursuers cannot pass, shaded by tulip poplar and beech, honeysuckle climbing over the log, reclaiming it for the soft earth. There is a worn patch of wood midway down the trunk shining silver grey in the sun, a place where the bark has been worn away by many feet, by the bodies of untold children clambering over it, the seats of their pants worn thin, polishing the wood to a dull sheen. You see this one spot of silver in so much green and watch it grow further away and so you run harder, the leaves of corn slapping at your arms, the damp air clinging to your skin and filling you with the smells of the earth in constant decay, the reek of nature consuming itself like some insane invalid chewing on its own toes and just as you're closing in on the one grey patch of sanity on the horizon you notice that vines have climbed over it and dragged it back into the woods, but all the time you know you'll make it over; to think anything less—to only wish to get there— would never be enough. We are crossing over this boundary every day, my brother and I, but we are always alone, and I think it is not so different for you, perhaps, digging through this tangle of memory and dream, like Penelope at her loom, unravelling and weaving the events of our lives, an hour lost in the thick woods, a vision through the crack of a door, an afternoon spent with our heads bowed, picking at the loose threads of a worn couch, listening to a man cataloguing our faults in a room that is too warm. We are all at work, bent across our looms, pulling apart these threads of memory, following them into the dark, into the open country beneath our ribs, running as hard as we can through the green leaves and the soft earth sinking beneath us.

Perhaps you had a grandfather and he sat you down from time to time on a couch you can never forget, its velvet arms worn smooth and reeking of cigarettes and old people, a few patches of velvet still clinging to the arm of the couch and it reminded you of moss on the rocks down by the creek where you would have rather been. And would still rather be, lying on a flat rock jutting out into the water, your chin resting on an island of moss, waiting for a crayfish to come out from under the rock, your hand poised in the water numb and ghost-like beneath you, too big to belong to you, but somewhere deep in the woods or in the leaves overhead his voice keeps rumbling on, "oh rosy fingered dawn carrying coal every morning in the wheelbarrow...too small to push a full load up the hill and so...in half-loads...and the moon those nights on the Brandywine...the sergeant said I was a marksman...holding that boy down with his leg half off...the smell of gangrene one needed," as Homer said, "*a heart hard as iron,*" and he would read on and on about "*the wine dark sea the waves that will race to shore long after Troy has vanished and so they burned Hector, breaker of horses...*" droning on, never in his own words, but carrying even into the thickest brambles and branches overhead, insisting that you return to the room with the couch and books lining the wall, *The Rise and Fall of Someone...Plutarch's This and Such Ad Nauseam* so that years later it makes you want to gather up all of those books, the catalogues of shortcomings and proud Hector himself and set a match to the lot, the old couch and Grandpa droning on through the flames. It's not such an unusual thought really, to set the old man on fire, an unravelling we all need to accomplish before we can cross over a boundary into the deep woods, the figures that need to burn or dissemble before we let ourselves have what we want so much we've never allowed ourselves to even think it for fear it would be taken from us.

I sit here casting words out into space in hopes that as they land we can see something of the shape of what lies beneath, a silhouette of this terrain we are running into. Already there are vague figures rising up like trees at the side of a dark path: the shadow of an old man, a book written in a dead tongue that no one ever really spoke to begin with, a war in which men finally became so efficient at killing—and even more so at dying—that they shocked even themselves. A year into the Great War, the German emperor was rumored to have said when viewing the bodies of the dead and wounded, "I did not want this to happen."

Does this approach seem unprofessional to you? Would you prefer that I disguise the issues at hand, create a young protagonist (cleverly disguised as myself) or develop a plot in which we follow the grandfather as an idealistic youth through the war to see what tragic event scarred his young psyche. I hope you aren't disappointed, knowing this story is being written, a weaving seen from the backside, full of knots and loose ends, frayed edges unravelling into memories only you possess, meanings only you can assign to the connections between my grandfather's life and the Great War, your grandfather and a book written 2,700 years ago by whom—the historians can't seem to agree, a blind man or woman or a committee of blind men, none of whom could write, dictating the whole story while scribes bent over leather or rolls of papyrus—imagine how long that would take: months of cramped scribbling over a period of years, a great cave full of old men and women talking at the same time, the echo of quills or bones scratching while the words fell onto the page like autumn leaves, like snow in a country where it had never snowed before, the room finally quiet as the last one said, *"and so died Hector, breaker of horses,"* and all of this, the men, women, the great cave, all in a language that no one spoke, even then.

This story too is written in a dead language; without you it would remain nothing but black scratches on a white page. It is my gift to you, an alchemical codex with which you reinterpret the experiences of your life, black seeds on the page waiting for water: the dream you had last night, the stories your grandfather or mother told you or didn't, the way you feel when the first snow comes spinning out of a grey sky to melt on your tongue, all the intricacies of your life that make me wonder who you are. You're an attentive reader, of course, but even more important I know I can depend upon you to be inattentive, to drift on currents this story only sets in motion.

These words I am setting down are an act of dreaming and as you pick them up I hope they will help you dream. In this place it is green everywhere and I am no longer running; I slow to a walk and stand listening for footsteps. I turn in the soft earth and look behind me. There is a green hill of corn marching in neat rows, and behind it is another green hill. I can't remember why I was running. I walk until the old log disappears behind me into the woods. The ground is getting softer. I am walking out into no man's land. I step on something hard in the soil; it's a bayonet, the blade cut with jagged teeth—for producing more horrible wounds?—no, for cutting firewood. Every regiment had one, for building fires against the cold and wet when they were back of the lines where it was permissible to build fires. I am walking into no man's land because it is one of the things behind me; it is a part of the alchemical codex I am trying to unravel. Some of it is encoded in fragments of conversation: my aunt once said to me, "Your grandfather went into that war as an idealistic young man and something happened to him there." My grandfather once said, about my uncle and father, with genuine surprise still in his voice, "The river boat pilot became a lawyer, and the lawyer became a river boat pilot." My father could have said the same about my brother and myself. I am walking over this hill to see how a thing like that could happen again, to see if there is some connection between the Great War and these green hills rolling through my dreams over and over again, rolling unchecked from one generation to the next, to see if there is any other way through this place. I am taking soundings, looking out for shoals, gathering testimony, accumulating research for a brief. I am not taking any chances. I will use anything I find that will get me out of here. I still have the bayonet.

He's sitting in a field of poppies. Almost everywhere, as far as the eye can see, the ground is carpeted red. Here and there cornflowers bristle up as blue as his eyes. Where the earth shows through it is heaped up in mounds or hollowed-out craters, scarred grey and yellowish by bombs. This is what it looks like behind the lines in spring in this part of France; the front moves forward a few hundred yards and the disturbed earth left behind is overrun with wildflowers. I don't remember in which part of France my grandfather was stationed. I'm sure he told me, but I've forgotten and he's dead now. My brother thinks it was someplace that begins with an S.

The trenches are only half a mile away. They are grey and brown, full of water, mud, lice, straw, men standing up to their ankles in water; the acrid stench of explosives and decaying flesh seeps in through the barbed wire. My grandfather guessed that in the no man's land between the trenches there were 7,000 corpses per square mile. "Your nose," he said, "told you where they lay the thickest." The German lines were a hundred and fifty yards away. I have checked on this and what he says is true; all the descriptions say that. They say they could hear the Bosches singing at night with their accordions, smell their cigar smoke drifting in on the breeze, unscathed by the coils and coils of barbed wire. I don't know about the bodies. I have no reason to doubt him; it's what he did, collect bodies, the dead ones and the ones who weren't quite finished. He said that during a shelling the ones they'd buried in shallow graves were often unearthed again, that part of the debris that rained down into the trenches was often flesh. He said the flowers surprised him. He often thought, after a day of carrying the wounded out of the field, of driving his ambulance through the craters and mud and carrion—for they were no longer human in his mind—that after a day like that it didn't seem possible that the flowers could still be there, only a few hundred yards behind the lines.

His uniform is covered in mud. From a distance he looks immaculate, sitting bolt upright in his field chair, his book open before him, but now I can see that he isn't even reading at all. The pages are fluttering in the wind.

There is a gulf between the words marching across the pages of *The Iliad* and the mud of no man's land, the limbs twisted against the skyline in a stunted forest of flesh and bone and the flash and splendor of the bronze-clad Achaeans marching into battle, their forest of spears standing straight and noble against the walls of Troy. I have no way of knowing if my grandfather saw such a gulf. In fact, I am almost certain he saw no such thing at all—perhaps that book was the one thing between him and the men he held down in the operating rooms crying for their homes, shitting their beds, screaming for an end to whatever was happening to them—and so he sits in his field of poppies, remembering the swift-footed Achaeans and strong-greaved Trojans, Hector, tamer of horses, and Achilles, burning and yet somehow still cold in his rage. What right do I have to take that from him, this idea he had that he was engaged in something noble, something bigger than himself. He told me once that I was the eldest and that there would be times when I would have to do what I had to do and for no other reason. I sat there on that old couch that still is the smell of old people for me today and I watched the islands of moss growing on its velvet arms while he told me about what he did in the war. I remember that couch better than I remember my grandfather. I remember that he said his job one day was to hold down a boy whose leg had become infected from the standing water in the trenches. The infection had gone unattended, so he was suffering from gangrene. I didn't know what that meant; I still have no clear idea, except that it smells. My grandfather told me that. "It's a smell you don't ever want to know," he said. The leg had to come off and the boy didn't want to lose his leg so he was crying and begging my grandfather to not let them take off his leg. The doctor was out of the room for some tool of his trade and the boy was begging my grandfather to get him the hell out of there and then when the doctor came back he started moaning and rocking back and forth so that my grandfather could barely hold him down, all the time making these noises, braying in a way humans should never be allowed to sound and shitting his pants while my grandfather held him down because it was what he had to do, he said, it was what he had to do.

I don't know anything about war. I have never been in one and I have done what little I could to say that it is not alright with me. I have stood on street corners with pathetic little signs whining to no one in particular and I have been arrested in carefully orchestrated displays for the press, and I have heard the stories from men I have worked with on construction sites, standing over a propane heater and watching the snow outside while they talk about the jungle and some spray they dropped from planes so that the plants all grew too fast so that they kill themselves from growing so much and so hard—this was agent orange and you knew there was something about it even then that wasn't right, they said, walking through the dead zones, everything dead from having grown too much. I believe this because these are men I admit I respect, knowing full well that is not something one admits to these days when people think themselves mature simply by being cynical. I have read the accounts and listened to the slurred ranting of men I would not want in my home, but I have never been there. I have never been there, but I do know one thing, that the way that boy screamed for his leg is not the way men died in *The Iliad*. They went down noble and clean, like trees in the forest: *and down the Trojan fell as an oak or a white poplar falls or towering pine that shipwrights up on a mountain hew down with whetted axes for sturdy ship timber—so he stretched in front of his team and chariot, sprawled and roaring, clawing the bloody dust.* I am no closer to understanding what comfort my grandfather got from that book in so much mud and shit and blood, the shells exploding and the sound of bullets so familiar that he could distinguish the low hum of a Mannlicher from the whine of a Springfield, but I know Achilles would not have stood for any of the grovelling that boy did in his bed: "*So friend, you die also. Why all this clamor about it? Patroklus also is dead, who was better by far than you are. Do you not see what a man I am, how huge, how splendid and born of a great father, and the mother who bore me immortal? Yet even I have also my death and my strong destiny, and there shall be a dawn or an afternoon or a noontime when some man in the fighting will take the life from me also either with a spearcast or an arrow flown from the bowstring. "* So he spoke, and in the other the knees and the inward heart went slack. He let go of the spear and sat back, spreading wide both hands; but Achilles drawing his sharp sword struck him beside the neck at the collar-bone, and the double-edged sword plunged full-length inside. He dropped to the ground face downward, and lay at length, and the black blood flowed, and the ground was soaked with it.* So who am I to disturb my grandfather, sitting there bolt upright with his one corner of sanity spread out in his lap, his muddy uniform, the last light of day soaking into the red-black poppies.

My grandfather wanted to be a marksman. That was his one great disappointment of the war, that he never had the opportunity to shoot the way he knew he could. Back in the States at boot camp they showed all of the men how to clean and fire their rifles. My grandfather was especially adept at target practice. His sergeant told him he was a marksman, but when the time came to move overseas they were divided up according to the way they were needed: the first twenty guys went into the infantry and the next twenty guys became ambulance drivers, the next twenty gunners, oiling down howitzers and covered in grease for the duration of the war. Once, on a day of leave, he'd gotten the idea to go and see General Pershing himself about his dilemma, and he had gotten as far as G.H.Q. without anyone stopping him. He imagined Black Jack as a towering man in gold brocade and epaulets, with a sword on his belt. He thought he might run into the general as he went out to review the troops on his horse. Grandpa had always been crazy over horses, especially those in *The Iliad*, breathing fire and running four abreast with a chariot behind them. The only thing better than being a marksmen would to have been to ride in the cavalry; he probably thought he would get a commission to ride with Pershing into battle like Patroclus and Achilles, charging into battle in their chariots, casting their bronze-tipped spears at the enemy.

He never saw Pershing that day. He wandered around a series of barracks that he was told was general headquarters, but he never saw a field map stretched out with markers showing positions, or any of the paraphernalia he imagined he would find. Instead, from all the barracks he heard what he first took to be rain falling on a tin roof, or pebbles landing on the floor. It turned out to be the sound of typewriters, clacking away in steady waves, twenty or more of them in each barrack. He stumbled away shaking his head, and years later he would tell my brother and I it wasn't any sort of war they were running there; it had been more like a secretarial pool at Sears and Roebuck. And so he had given up on the idea of changing his job in such a bureaucracy and went about his work, bringing in the wounded and holding them down while they were treated or until they were too weak to fight any longer. By the end of the war he saw his work in the ambulance corps as essential to the war effort. In addition to carrying off the wounded, as medical personnel he was supposed to help teach the men proper hygiene. The only way to prevent trench foot, which could lead to gangrene if not treated, was to clean and dry one's feet daily, and so the men were ordered to change socks on a regular basis. Socks were hardly ever available, however, and the men often stood in cold water for the entire stretch of their six-day watch. Furthermore, fires would draw enemy artillery attacks. In the winter of 1918, his battalion of 12,000 at S_____ had been decimated by dysentery, trench foot, influenza, and trench fever carried by lice and rodents. By the end of that winter, 6,000 men had been lost to non-combat illness or death.

When my grandfather died I helped my father carry his things down into the basement. I think my father was ashamed of the way Grandpa died, alone and in a nursing home. I am not sure I should be writing this down. It is a dangerous business, digging through memory; one never knows just how much to lie to oneself to get at a truth. I'm trying to clarify boundaries, to ascertain the lines between privacy and events that never took place, obvious lies that somehow come too close to the truth, so raw that it seems criminal to let outsiders read it. My grandfather refused to buy my father glasses, even though as a little boy he was blind as a bat. My grandfather wanted him to stay home and read books, to keep him out of the streets; he lived in constant fear that my father might be run over by a street car and so he kept him at home until one day when he was nine or ten and the neighbors were over on the front porch admiring the bright orange feathers of a baltimore oriole in the lilac bushes alongside the house. Where, said my father, where's the bird? I want to see it, until he became panicked at the thought that everyone could see this bright flame darting through the bushes but him. Only then did my grandfather take him to get glasses.

I write down everything that I think I shouldn't write down; if I am ever going to learn anything from pieces of blank paper I can keep nothing from them. I know it sounds incredible, but I actually believe this. My father was ashamed of himself for the way my grandfather died, and my grandfather was ashamed of my father for not going to fight when it came his turn. What did my grandfather think of Odysseus, that most ingenious of draft dodgers, sowing his fields with salt? And when the messenger placed Odysseus' son in the way of the plow, did my grandfather cringe? Did my grandfather think, how can a man do that to another man, ask him to run down his son to prove his madness, ask him how much he was willing to pay to stay out of that dirty war, one man after another man's property, because let's be honest, Helen was many things, but most of all she was property. Who can blame Odysseus, after all, for not wanting to fight in Menelaos' dirty little war over pussy. Yes pussy, pelt, cunt, all those dirty little words that transform the living, breathing Helen into so much coin in Menelaos' pocket, because, let's cut through some of this smoke and mirrors about the complexity of war: it is always about power, the greedy taking what they want, whether they call it making the world safe for making a buck or the winning of souls, it is all just so much coin falling into the hollow spaces we all carry inside us that can never be filled.

How did we get here, from my father's basement to this whining about war? These sentences have grown wild, a mat of tendrils crawling off in all directions. Some of them have been pruned back and you will never see them. These may be more important than the ones left behind. Isn't this how we read, following tangents off into the dark, following my father down his cellar stairs, carrying an old trunk that never existed down into the dark? To his credit, my father never feigned madness to get out of his war, but my grandfather never forgave him for that. It was a failing he could never erase, a standard like so many others my grandfather set which could never be known, let alone attained.

Grandpa brought the trunk back from the Great War. I'm not sure what I expected to discover: spiked helmets or bayonets, secret love letters to a mistress. I should have known better; my grandfather was not the kind of man who trafficked in souvenirs. When I opened the lid I was wrapped in the smell of damp wool and leather. I could almost feel it scratching against my skin, wrapped in his smell and those layers and layers of talks on the old couch. There were books and and his mess kit and uniform, and in the bottom was an old belt spotted with mold, a canteen case, press clippings bound up with a few letters, yellow and faded to the point that they were almost illegible. The clippings were nothing remarkable, the usual "Give the Kaiser Hell" and "Peace at Last," but the letters were something else. As near as I can piece together, they must have belonged to men who'd asked my grandfather to deliver them; along with the bundle I found a list of addresses in his cramped handwriting, with new additions and older entries scratched out. Some were addresses in France and England, but most were from the States. He even had one in German, which I have had a friend translate; this fellow must have been a prisoner of war who'd been treated in the field hospital. Grandpa apparently spent most of his life trying to track down their families, and these leftovers are the forever lost. My grandfather had been carrying out this great humanitarian campaign for years without any of us knowing his secret. Here is some of what

I found: *New Year's Eve was quite strange. An English officer appeared with a white flag and asked for a truce between eleven and three for burying the dead (shortly before Christmas there had been violent enemy attacks in which the English had lost many dead and wounded). It was granted. It is good not to see the corpses lying around anymore. The truce was then extended. The English came out of their trenches, and midway, cigarettes, also photographs were exchanged. They said they did not want to shoot any more. So there was an absolute quiet that struck you as strange. It could not go on this way, so we sent word they should return to their trenches, as we would shoot. Then the officer said he was sorry, but his men did not obey him. They said they could not lie any longer in those wet trenches, and that France was gone. Actually, they are much dirtier than we, have more water in their trenches and many sick. They are mercenaries, so they just go on strike. Of course, we did not shoot. Does the whole English army strike, spoiling the game of those gentlemen in London?* Karl Aldag, German student, letter of January 3, 1915.

If you wish to appreciate the nature of trench warfare in winter, find a piece of wet, flat country, dig a ditch seven or eight feet deep and stand in icy water staring across at another ditch, and sleep in a cellar that you have dug in the wall of course, the moist walls will be continually falling in and require mending in a drenching, freezing rain of the kind the Lord visits on all who wage war underground in Flanders. Incidentally, you must look after the pumps, lest the water rise to your neck then, arrange some bags of bullets with dynamite charges on the wire and sink heavier charges under your feet, which will do for mines—and set them off, while you engage someone to toss grenades and bombs at you. Frederick Palmer, on trench warfare in Flanders, January 1915.

The faster I read the slower Grandpa reads in his red field, cold and unhurried, or perhaps it's only the wind turning pages under a cloudy sky, a litany of words passing overhead like clouds, rising up clear as notes of music over the noise of the field, words invoked with inhuman calm: *Achilles was closing on him now, like the god of war, the fighter's helmet flashing, over his right shoulder shaking the Pelian ash spear, that terror, and the bronze around his body flared like a raging fire or the rising, blazing sun he reared and jammed his lance through the man's ear so the lance came jutting out through the other ear, bronze point glinting. Echelus, son of Agenor next—Achilles split his head at the brow with hilted sword so the whole blade ran hot with blood, and red death came plunging down his eyes, and the strong force of fate.*

The messroom presented a ghastly sight this morning, a hand grenade having been accidentally exploded, blowing two men to bits, which bits are still hanging to the walls. Robert Whitney Imbrie at Cappy, France, April, 1918.

Deucalion next—he lanced his arm with a bronze-shod spear, he spitted the Trojan through where the elbow tendons grip and there he stood, waiting Achilles, arm dangling heavy, staring death in the face and Achilles chopped his neck and his sword sent head and helmet flying off together and marrow bubbling up from the clean-cut neckbone. Down he went, his corpse full length on the ground—just as Achilles charged at Pira's handsome son, Rhigmus who had sailed from the fertile soil of Thrace—Achilles pierced his belly, the bronze impaled his guts and out of his car he pitched as his driver Areithous swung the horses round but Achilles speared his back and the spearshaft heaved him off the chariot too and the panicked stallions bolted.

Oh these horrible minutes! One is afraid to die, and during such hours one could long for death out of fear to die in this fashion. I have been in two assaults. May there not be another one! Where did all the courage go? We had enough of waging war. One does not have to be a coward, but humane sentiment revolts against this barbarity, this gruesome slaughter. Finish this war, finish it as quickly as possible! Kurt Peterson, German student, letter to his parents, October, 1914.

"Come friend, you too must die. Why moan about it so? Even Patroklus died, a far, far better man than you."

Got a copy of New Republic, *Pacifist leanings. Most of army has, too. War spirit in inverse ration to proximity of war. Quickest way to end it, put all journalists and politicians under arms. Leave peace arrangements to soldiers, under rank of Lieut. Make talkers fight and fighters talk.* H.V. O'Brien, diary, March 1918.

Achilles now like inhuman fire raging on through the mountain gorges splinter-dry, setting ablaze big stands of timber, the wind swirling the huge fireball right and left—chaos of fire—Achilles storming on with brandished spear like a frenzied god of battle trampling all he killed and the earth ran with black blood. Thundering on, on like oxen broad in the brow some field hand yokes to crush white barley heaped on a well-laid threshing floor and the grain is husked out fast by the bellowing oxen's hooves—so as the great Achilles rampaged on, his sharp-hooved stallions trampled shields and corpses, axle under his chariot splashed with blood, blood on the handrails sweeping round the car, sprays of blood shooting up from the stallions hooves and churning, whirling rims—and the son of Peleus charioteering on to seize his glory, bloody filth splattering both strong arms, Achilles invincible arms—

I see my grandfather driving his ambulance over the fields, the axle mired in mud, mud splashing up from the ruts and potholes, tires spinning up the low greasy hills. My aunt says that on a day like this he once helped some men to pull a horse from the mud. Perhaps he was thinking of Achilles, of his fierce stallions churning into battle, blood flecking their steaming flanks, their strong jaws foaming white as waves breaking on the beach of Troy. The road traversing no man's land dipped down into a bog before it climbed the rise toward the German lines. It was a stream of mud crawling down into the reeds, an impenetrable fen of brambles and trees, and over the winter it had become a depository of equipment, fragments of weapons and men. These were the last months of the war; the Germans had given up another few hundred meters of tortured earth. My grandfather was driving across the reclaimed no man's land to pick up the wounded and bring them back behind the lines. The horse had been hauling a wagon of some sort, full of parts of vehicles and machinery worth scavenging, and had gotten stuck crossing the bog. My grandfather needed to get through so he stopped to help pull the horse out. He was only a caricature of a horse, actually, all bones and loose skin, smeared green and brown in algae and filth from rolling in the pit. He lay on his side, submerged in the mud, panting from the effort of trying to stand. He would struggle almost to his feet and then roll onto the opposite side. It reminded me of a soldier Grandpa had befriended in the field hospital. I got the feeling that Grandpa kept a certain distance from most of the men he carried in, but this fellow was altogether different. Sometimes my grandfather went into the trenches after a battle, searching for the wounded; there were mazes down there, sections built underground and zigzags running off in every direction. He found this fellow kneeling in the trench, trying to stand up. As my grandfather approached him he gave him a crooked salute and keeled over into the mud. He told my grandfather later that the worst part of being wounded was that when his commanding officer had come through the lines he hadn't been able to stand up and greet him properly. Their position had been shelled and he'd been knocked down by the shock of the blast but hadn't actually been hit. He told my grandfather that the one thing that kept bothering him was that he couldn't get to his feet and salute; he could get to his knees, but as soon as he raised up his head the world began to reel and the next thing he knew he was laying on his stomach in the dirt again. In his delirium he kept trying to get to his feet again and again, until his trench mates convinced him to lie still. He'd somehow fixated on this as being very important, to get to his feet and salute, and it still bothered him that he was unable to do so. He was the one man wounded in the war my grandfather sympathized with, a man willing but unable to do what he had to do. Perhaps he thought of his friend as he watched the horse slump into the mud; perhaps he simply wanted the horse out of his way so he could get on with his job, but I think most of all he did it just because he liked horses and it was an event taking place on a scale he could do something about, and so he waded out into the bog with a shovel to the men working there. The horse had evidently gotten its legs caught under a log or some piece of equipment and the men were trying to dig him out as best they could. There were four of them down there in the mud with pry bars and shovels, the horse kicking out at anyone dumb enough to get behind it, braying in a voice that sounded almost human. They thought the first corpse was the trunk of a tree, stiff as it was under the mud and sewage of the bog, and as the horse continued to thrash and travel downstream in the pit they found two more, tangled and trampled in the hooves of the horse, so contorted and fixed in their poses that they might have been stumps pulled out of the bog if it weren't for the lacerations from the horse and the smell. And still the damned horse kept thrashing out at the men, its bone eyes shining wild, almost as if it were accusing them of some kind of betrayal. It would not be calmed or helped out of the bog, though my grandfather clung to its neck and whispered, "There now, that's a good fella, there now. There now," soft and sweet while it raged and foamed at the mouth, a yellow bile covering Grandpa's hands and chest with a smell he could never rid himself of, even years later. "Let's shoot the damn thing," one said, and the others agreed, except Grandfather, who would have none of it. One by one they all got the hell out of the mud to let the thing die, but my grandfather stayed in with it, lying in the shit and blood and stench of corpses with a goddamn broken, good-for-nothing horse, lying there all that night in the cold and wet crawling into him, staring up at the stars which didn't give a damn about him or the horse. He lay there all that night and of this I am certain: he lay there and he cried. He cried over that damn horse, he who told us there was no such thing as emotions—or at least so my aunt says—my father says he never so much as mentioned the word to him. It was a thing you could only talk about to a woman, and then only to say it did not exist.

I see him sitting in the meadow in back of the lines, after his buddies dragged him the hell out of there and got him back to the field hospital where they cleaned him up as best they could, after he put on his uniform next morning same as always, every button done up to the top and his spats in place, still spattered in mud and reeking of that horse, after going to mess as if nothing had happened, never touching the food on his plate and no one saying a word to him, after he walked out into that field of poppies with his damn book as if it was what he did every day, as if that were his job, to sit in this field in back of the lines, the land he told me they'd reclaimed for France and democracy. I see him sitting there all day long, taking no food or drink, saying nothing to anyone while the day burns on and on, those poppies growing too fast like the jungles of Vietnam, surging up in red waves to lick at the soft underbellies of the clouds.

I remember lying on a moss-covered rock deep in the woods. I was waiting for a crayfish to come out from under the rock. I remember my grandfather's arms scooping me up and carrying me home, his voice still carrying down through the branches, carrying me home to do what I have to do. I remember my grandfather giving my mother money after my father had gone away, telling me I was the oldest now, I had to look after my mother, I had to look after my brother and my sisters. How does one look after so many people? He used to take me hiking, into the mountains, into the deep smell of fir balsam and spruce, and I remember the piles of hair falling to the floor, the snip of the barber's scissors cutting the air each time before I went into the mountains with my grandfather. Such simple things: afternoons spent sitting on an old couch, stiff words falling off our shoulders like hair—how can they hem us in—little islands of hair on the floor, voices echoing through branches, through a great cave, many voices misremembering the same event, all in a language that was never spoken. What do they really matter now, after all these years?

A breeze trembles over the field in the near darkness, swelling through the deep red-black of the poppies. My grandfather looks out over the field toward no man's land and mouths the dead words, *"the wine dark sea, the waves that will race to shore long after Troy has vanished."* I wonder how he can still insist on his wine dark sea, surrounded as he is by so much blood. I wonder what happened to him that night lying out in the cold, if the ancient light of the stars sank right through him, marking him in a way that made everything he saw in that war somehow bearable, a sense of sidereal time and events unavailable to him in the labyrinth of trenches and dead ends he wandered searching for the wounded, a vision of calm and order in which the truth of great events proceeds inevitably forward like a great stone over the chaff of feelings and weak men crying for mercy, a vision that carried him forward but forever distant from his sons and daughters. There is no single night that can account for so much, no simple train of events that can be added together to equal a story, only dreams unravelling what we thought we knew. I can barely make him out now, sitting bolt upright in his chair, like Odysseus lashed to the mast, clutching his book against the voices of sirens, the incoming waves of darkness. There is hardly anything left of him. I wonder why it is I still hate him so much, even after all these years.

Author's note: all selections from *The Iliad* are from Robert Fagle's 1990 translation from Viking Press. German student letters are from Phillip Witkop's *German Students' War Letters*, E.P. Dutton, 1929. All "Allied" letters are from Joe Kirchberger's *The First World War: An Eyewitness History, Facts on File*, 1992.

Leaf or Tongue
Matthew Cooperman

for Tristina

There is a tree that begins each day with its own rustling. Back and forth, back and forth, it begs to be personified. Yet it keeps on at the very ordinary pace that it keeps on. Hopeful, perhaps, or it is nice to think so, and in the spring it will throw up its green flame like a diva's voice that speaks in another language. Another language. What were we about to say? Mouths open, each time, is this our voice? My daughter cries. The son I do not have asks for instruction; how to glue the bumper on the black van, or, do skeletons go to heaven just like angels? You wait, the silent second person, beginning, beginning...and the tree moves. Now its leaves are out. Now you say, *wait, stop, look in my perfect green eyes*. We can go on like this with our reading and hand-building. The person changes each day, but the wish is the same. The tree knows this with its perfect history of veins and possible branchings, and no matter how hard I think my way into color I will never turn red or gold, never learn to drop myself helically from the highest branch. In the morning we go our separate ways. The wind begins to say. Speaking for the other or not speaking at all.

Akhmatova
Amy Scattergood

For forty years,
as the armies of the state boxed up the country
in bone factories
and gunfire

perforated the censored sky,
she committed poetry
to memory, her own
and the seven other people she could trust

not to recite it
to government spies.
People could disappear forever
for a fragment of paper,

a few lines.
Under samovar lids
and cataclysms of Shostakovich
she'd take inventory

to make sure
nothing deteriorated. The ditches of her memory
suffered.
She'd spent eighteen years in line

outside Leningrad prisons
with other blue-lipped women
traceable
in storm outlines.

Now she moves
through blind houses
with her invisible poetry, whispering
the secret archives in pieces

for precaution, listening
as different voices repeat
the rhymes
like grocery lists

and ragged feet
tap out the meters under cardboard tables.
Forty years of poetry
transcribed in coffee stains

and bread lines
like codes
hidden from shaken lightbulbs and telephones and neighbors.
What discipline it must have taken

not to get lost in the fragmentation
and disappear
into the sugar bowls and potato skins
without paper to remember her.

How many nights,
leaning into the storm cloud
shuttles from Siberia,
her memory must have threatened to

shut down—the censors
erasing her mind while she slept—
except for the blue-lipped women at the gates whispering
language (remember this) is older than state.

Dreams of Empire
Amy Scattergood

How the trees repeat themselves
and the horizon rolls over to begin again.
Discovery's conceit is believing no one has been here before.
    We took up the land like carpeting.

The horizon rolls and begins again:
a caravan of hills, birch trees blown to bone.
We took up the land like carpeting
    as if the houses were already there.

(A caravan of hills. The trees blown to bone.)
Above us a carapace of broken stars.
As if the houses were already there,
    we heard the night like an outside sentry walking.

Beneath a carapace of broken stars,
it's easy to lose your grasp of the surroundings.
Listen to the night like an outside sentry walking
    then project (if you can) the round earth on a square map.

It's so easy to lose your grasp of the surroundings
as the weather like armies moves among us.
Project the round earth on a square map:
    find the latitude; measure the migration of the sun.

As weather like armies moves among us,
try to locate the stars, choose a direction,
find some latitude or measure the migration of the sun.
    But the sky has dropped to a blank white page.

Locate the stars or just choose a direction
because the landscape does not stop when you do.
(The sky dropping to a blank white page,
    the birds writing across the sky.)

The landscape cannot stop when you do.
(Your bearings are gone, your hemisphere is turning,
the same birds are writing across the same sky.)
    The grass is moving to cover your tracks.

Your bearings gone, your hemisphere turning
(the conceit is believing no one has been here before),
watch as the grass moves to cover your tracks.
    As the trees keep repeating.

Infinite Odyssey Just before Closing Time
Christine L. Monahan

A snail-track of thumbs in dew
on that bare neck
of the bottle
through which he sees
islands,
glaciers,
and seas
of frozen days
dotting a horizon
divided
by night-aged eyes,
while numb lips try a push-up against the force of air, firm as the floor
under the foot
anchoring him to the room,
keeping him near his lady-in-
waiting to be kissed
by the questing tongue
still engaged in noble duel
with dragons that live
in the coastline
of smoke.

Having Been Removed from You, I
Christine L. Monahan

am haunted by warmth, like day-weary clothes, abandoned by the touch of skin,

thrill

still lodged in the neck,
long past the crest of the road

-side jack rabbit
matted to steaming asphalt,
forgotten,
even by pursuing wolves,

black behind the eyes,
blank sleep
deprives
of a soapy wash of dreams, and you,

indwelling figure, emerge
from marble
as I am
what is cut away,
and falls
like colorless wings
of the broken moth.

A Letter Home
Linda Nowlin

I think constantly of nothing. Nothing
you would think of import: imported trinkets,
batiks from India, India ink, rice-paper poems,
poems written in exile, in retreat.

I think relentlessly, constantly,
of inconsistency, the inconsistency
of an opera singer's vowels, a vocalized sound,
dialects, drawls, their pitch and key.

One day I throw mad, wild Italian kisses
to a sea of radios, to an avocado in a cave.
And the next day, I squeeze a lemon
so full of lust it could stun you to silence.

Mother, I see your hands shaking. But
if you were desperate—you too, might paint
scorpions blue. You too, might pity the strut
of the satyr confined in a hotel dumbwaiter.
You, too, might sleep in a sea of radios,
toss roses from a balcony in Brazil,
to no one, into a river of dreams, into sky.

Car Love
Linda Nowlin

My mother married a man who was in love
with his auto. The second day after he came,
he moved a bed to the garage so he could watch
his car and sleep. Mother didn't seem to mind.
What, after all, could she do?

He liked getting dirty, staying dirty. The smell
of grease in his jumpsuit, smudges around his nose,
under his nails. Who could argue if dirt on his dark face
made him happy? People would sigh, shake their heads,
say, *My, what a drive your big Daddy has.*

Some nights, he wouldn't let me near him—
yelling with his fists raised in Moses fashion.
he even put mirrored tiles all over one wall.
Then he would rub cream onto the fenders, and watch
the wax sealing in what was rich, luminous and pure.

Some days, it was all he could do just to scrub
the car, the soap foaming around his hands.
*It just takes a bit, but look at it, girl,
look at all them tons of bubbles.* And I looked—
at fingers corroded past any notion of pain.

Nights, I'd go to kiss him and see him
reflected in the mirror, in the pale blue fenders,
the silver hubcaps going around. His big toes
curled and hugged his bed, rocking the mattress,
as he told tales of his adventures: the carnivals,
casinos, the Casanova nights.

One day I found him, cocoon-like in his car,
and saw another day trip with his lips collapsing
in a dangerous grin, the engine revving one last time,
the shifting, the jamming gears, the burning
to go somewhere too far to make it back again.

Articles of Faith
Elizabeth Oness

Sometimes Terry imagined her answering machine was willfully silent, swallowing her most important messages. She pictured it swelling like a frog: the flat, rectangular box bulging into a convex shape, the lid popping open with the final suppressed call. She lay on her bed, a fold-out sofa, flipping through the *Village Voice*. She studied the Mind/Body/Spirit section, the personals; she told herself to get out, see a movie, maybe the phone would ring if she stopped watching it. The small sounds of the building, heat knocking in the pipes, Mrs. Andersson shuffling in and out, George talking baby-talk to his poodle outside her door, were magnified by the phone's silence.

Finally she gave in, grabbed her coat, and walked the five flights downstairs. Three days ago she had been called back for a part in a movie—not a walk-on, a real part. On the brownstone steps she hesitated, tapped her fingers against her mouth. "This is stupid, the phone is not broken," she told herself. Damp cold seeped up through her shoes. She pulled her coat more tightly around her and ran to the pay phone on the corner. Through the scratched plastic, she saw cloudy people hurrying against the wind. After four rings, her own voice answered; filtered through machinery, she sounded business-like, serene. She dropped the receiver into the cradle and stared out into the street. The city was littered with tired Christmas decorations and slush.

The past few days kept playing over in her mind. She had been in the shower when they called. The phone rang and she had turned to let the hot water run over her face. She imagined it was someone from the restaurant, calling because another waitress hadn't shown up, but then she heard a crisp, unfamiliar voice leaving a message on her machine, and she jumped out of the shower and fumbled for the phone. The woman, a casting agent for Paramount, was calling to say the director would like to hear her read. For a moment Terry thought it was a joke. Who would do this? She couldn't imagine. She'd sent off an audition tape months ago. The woman's voice, calm and impersonal, instructed Terry to pick up a script at an office in midtown. Terry scrabbled for something to write on and finally grabbed a Chinese take-out menu; water dripping from her hair smudged the ink and she had to ask the woman to repeat everything twice. When Terry hung up the phone, her apartment looked unfamiliar for a moment. It's only a callback, she told herself, wanting to quell the elation growing inside her. A part in a real movie. She saw herself in simple, elegant clothes, meeting with producers in high-rise offices instead of racing for the subway in a dress and heels, trying to avoid being splashed with slush. She would be plucked from the crowd. She thought of all those cattle-call auditions, competing with several hundred other women, trying not to arrive flushed, out of breath because the train had been delayed or she couldn't find the address, then cramming into a dirty bathroom to fix her hair or her makeup, trying not to poke the woman next to her with her elbow and create any more competitive hostility than they all already felt. When she called work to get out of her shift, Richie fired her. And this is what she has come to: standing in the street, listening to her own voice on her answering machine.

Climbing back up the stairs, she moved through the layered cooking smells that mingled on each landing: garlic on the second floor, something that smelled like cabbage on the third. She felt foolish for walking all the way down to check. Inside, she avoided looking for the light on her machine. Why didn't they call? Too ethnic-looking? It had been said before. She resembled her mother's family, all from southern Italy with dark hair and olive skin. These days she didn't bother to audition when they wanted an all-American type. Growing up, she wouldn't have known what ethnic meant; in Brooklyn, everyone came from somewhere. When she went to college upstate, she learned that there were WASPS, and other Americans were the hyphenated sort: Italian-American, African-American, Irish-American. When she started trying out for plays, she learned to accept being labeled as Mediterranean, just as she accepted that she was young and pretty. She could not accept her accent. At the movies, on television, she had learned what her voice implied—gum chewing, decaled fingernails, leopard-skin collar on the winter coat. By her sophomore year in college, she had smoothed her Brooklyn accent into a voice that was educated, unplaceable. She had set out to lose it in high school, knowing, even then, that her voice would always place her as a girl from Brooklyn. She spent hours in front of her bedroom mirror, watching her mouth as she tried to reshape its sounds: *new yawk, new yaawk*; she hated the mean-sounding vowels that inevitably formed in her mouth. She wanted to say "York," elegant and round, British-sounding, opening her mouth so the sound would become tall, spacious, the roof of her mouth a cathedral: *yawk, yaawk, yerk, york, York.* She'd never do Shakespeare if she sounded like the voices at home.

She flopped onto her open bed and kicked the Help Wanted section onto the floor. January was a lousy month to look for work. She walked over to the stack of Day-Glow plastic crates that served as her closet and pulled out the pieces of her job-hunting uniform: short skirt, black stockings, heels.

Out in the street, people were brightly wrapped against the cold. Everyone seemed to be carrying something: a hatless woman struggled down the street with a leafy houseplant, its greenness surprising in the gray air. Two clean-cut young men came out of the Erotic Baker, the smaller man carrying a white pastry box. She tried to imagine what was in the box, who they were bringing it to. She studied how people moved, how they walked and carried their shoulders, the various ways they negotiated the puddled curbs. Going to read for the director she'd felt purposeful, as if something large was being set in motion. She would look back and be able to pinpoint it—the part that changed everything. And it had happened just as she was beginning to lose faith. Studying acting was a filter through which she viewed her life: every feeling and reaction could be studied and used in the building of a character. The economy of using her life in this way pleased her, as if, and she knew this wasn't true, the living itself was not sufficient.

She walked down Columbus Avenue and inquired about jobs in any restaurant that looked promising. At Columbus and 74th, she walked under a bright awning that showed a man and a woman with cartoon balloons drawn above their mouths, "Italian? Argentine!" She walked in and asked the bartender about a waitressing job. He glanced at her, twisted a sheaf of cocktail napkins into a swirl, and set them on the bar. "I'll buzz the manager. Her name is Marie."

The dining room had white stuccoed walls and a fireplace at the back. Two men sat at a table in the corner, a bottle of red wine between them, talking quietly. Terry picked up a menu lying on the bar. Expensive steaks, grilled meats—if the food was good she could make some real money. A short, round woman with silvery hair hurried up to the bartender and, ignoring Terry, dropped a thick sheaf of papers on the bar.

"Tommy, some of these tickets don't match. And we're missing a case of Concha y Toro. The Cabernet Sauvignon."

She turned to Terry and looked her over without shaking her hand. Marie was a buxom woman, and in a bright, red blouse it was hard to tell where her breasts left off and the rest of her began. She asked Terry where she had worked, why she left. Terry didn't bother to lie.

"We need a pretty girl here. We had a girl, but she did too much coke and I fired her," Marie talked very fast, tapping her painted fingers on the bar. She reminded Terry of a yappy, overfed dog.

Marie led her down a hallway and into the back dining room. The late afternoon sun came through a skylight into a room that was unprepared, slightly dilapidated, like an unfinished set. Next to an espresso machine, a long table was covered with candles, stacks of red tablecloths, bales of linen napkins, and rows of cut-glass jars filled with unfamiliar sauces. A group of men sat at one end of another long table, talking and laughing over an afternoon meal. Marie poured herself a cup of coffee, said something in Spanish, and the men all turned to look at Terry. They nodded and smiled like a group of cousins at a wedding.

"Let me introduce you to Sergio, our chef," Marie waddled toward the kitchen and pushed through the swinging doors.

Sergio, a tall, thickset man in a white apron, greeted Terry by nodding in her direction. When he came forward to shake her hand, she saw his rhinestone earrings, large bright clusters set above studded strands of glass. Seeing Terry's gaze, he pursed his lips and patted his dark curly hair with his palm. Terry grinned.

"Sergio is temperamental, but he's a wonderful chef," Marie said. She patted his hairy arm, speaking as if he wasn't there.

"I will try to be patient while you are learning, but I must warn you," Sergio put his hands on his hips and Terry thought of a football player imitating a school teacher. "When a plate is ready, it must never wait. Only for this will I yell at you."

"Let me go over the menu with you," Marie said. "There are probably some things you'll need to know. You'll need to learn some Spanish if you're going to make it here."

Terry never had problems making herself understood. In the past, when a busboy or dishwasher didn't speak much English, she would pantomime what she needed. She tried to think of it as another acting exercise. But Marie had not been kidding; none of the busboys spoke any English. Juan, who'd been assigned to her section, merely grinned at her requests.

"Excuse me, miss, could we have some more water?" a customer asked.

She heard Sergio's bell. Her order for another table was up.

"Yes, of course," she smiled and looked around for Juan. She found him smoking a cigarette by the espresso machine.

"Juan, I need some water on table five."

He grinned. She held up a sweating water pitcher and pointed to the table where the man was sitting with his back to them. "*Agua*," she said.

Juan frowned and took a sip from his coffee cup. As he carried the pitcher of water toward her tables, Terry heard Sergio's bell again. Swinging out of the kitchen, she saw, from the corner of her eye, that Juan had started with the closest table in her section and topped off the water in every glass. He was nowhere near the man who had asked for it.

"I'm sorry," she said to him as she passed by. "I'll get the busboy right away."

She caught Juan's eye and nodded to the table where the man was waiting. Juan held up the empty pitcher triumphantly.

Terry served the food, got the water herself, then she crooked a finger at Juan and led him toward the back. "No tips. Can you understand that?" She looked straight at him, and his brown eyes grew large, surprised. A sullen expression thinned out his rosebud mouth. She knew he understood her, at least partially. "I'm not going to give you one fucking cent unless you take care of my tables the way you're supposed to." Her voice was quiet—she knew it was low to threaten such a thing. Even in anger, she was ashamed of her meanness.

One of the other busboys came up behind her. He said something quietly to Juan, who pouted and whisked the pitcher away.

"Juan, he is easier to make diplomacy with than push," the man's expression was grave, almost sorrowful. He had a round face with high cheekbones; in the dim light he looked almost Chinese. His hair was thick and straight, awkwardly cut into a helmet-like shape. The odd cut emphasized his features, which looking more closely, she saw were not Asian at all. He had deep-set eyes, a slightly flattened nose. Although he wasn't old, forty at most, the shape of his features seemed Indian, somehow ancient. Terry found herself staring; she couldn't read his expression.

"I'm sure you're right," Terry set down the tray she was clutching. "But it's like he's doing it on purpose, to bait me."

"Bait you?" he looked puzzled.

"Bait. Catch, like a fish," Terry explained.

"Oh, I do not think he wants to catch you," the busboy said seriously.

"I don't mean he wanted to catch me," Terry giggled. "I know Juan's not interested.

It's slang, sort of, for trying to trick someone, trying to make someone mad."

"I see," he closed his eyes for a moment, as if committing something to memory.

"What would help, with Juan, is to learn a little Spanish."

Terry glanced over at her tables. Juan was walking up and down ostentatiously, belly pushed out like a small child, the water pitcher in his hand.

"My name is Alberto," he made a little bow.

"I'm Terry."

"Teresa," he said solemnly. And looking over his shoulder, "I must go to my tables."

Every day she waited for the call. It seemed that a judgement was being made on the past ten years of her life. If she got the part, it meant that her persistence and hard work had paid off. And if she didn't? Did it mean that she'd been fooling herself? Hoping for something she didn't have the talent for? She'd seen a movie the other night about a basketball player who couldn't keep from gambling on himself. In different places she thought the movie was about to end, and it occurred to her, as she sat in the darkened theatre, that wherever the story ended determined what you thought about the character. If it ended when he was on a streak, then his bet had been worth it. If it ended when he was down, it meant he'd risked too much, once too many times. For her it was all one long gamble. She was thirty-two years old. She'd worked fairly consistently, more than a lot of people, but all the productions were in downtown performance spaces, off-off-off Broadway. She knew she was a better actress than she was ten years ago, but she had nothing to show for it except a mediocre resume and portfolio of head shots that made her look more glamorous than she was. When she wasn't acting, it was easy to convince herself that she was only a hopeful waitress, nothing more. She remembered coming home from college and telling her parents she'd be waitressing instead of getting a regular job.

"Four years of college and you want to wait tables?" her mother had said.

"Ma, I majored in drama. The whole idea of waitressing is so that when I get an acting job I can work around it."

"Why don't you teach? It's steady, good money. You go to college and become a waitress?"

Her father had watched them, faced off against each other, and when her mother turned to him to take her side, he would only smile. So they had relented, years ago, and her mother accepted her eldest daughter's floating life as a kind of transitory burden that would one day be laid to rest.

She had waited tables all over Manhattan, mostly with aspiring actors and actresses, hopeful writers and singers, all of them believing that their real lives lay elsewhere, all of them knowing how few of them would make it. There was an unspoken belief that the way their lives turned out would not only be a matter of talent and hard work, but finally there would be a deciding measure of luck or fate. And of course it was impossible to know how your luck would turn out unless you played to the end of your hand. This hadn't scared her when she was younger, but lately she had started to think that if success was not her fate, then it meant she was sacrificing a life of comfort and security for sleeping on a fold-out sofa, living in an apartment where the shower was in the kitchen, and what would remain, at the end of it all, would either be a romanticization of her past or an acknowledgement of its insignificance.

This waitressing job seemed different because most of the waiters and busboys had found at least part of what they wanted: they had made it to New York. Of course, once they arrived it wasn't easy. Many of the busboys were men, older than her. They lived in large numbers in small apartments in Queens; they worked several jobs to send money home.

One afternoon, after a hectic lunch and a small take on tips, she tapped Alberto on the arm.

"I've been thinking about what you said. I'd like to learn some Spanish."

"And you would teach some English also?"

He was so earnest. She studied him in the afternoon light, the fine wrinkles around his eyes, his tie still done up.

"You come to work one hour early tomorrow?" he asked.

"Well," she was surprised by his seriousness, "OK."

When she arrived at ten o'clock the following morning, Alberto was waiting, drinking a cup of coffee and looking at the *New York Times*. When he saw her come in, he got up to pour her coffee.

"Isn't the *New York Times* kind of hard to read?" she asked.

"I read better than talk," he said. "I study English in school, many years ago. Also, I think it is important to read the right paper, yes?"

"Well, I guess. *The Post* isn't exactly a class act."

He smiled, and she sensed that she had missed the point.

"In my country, it is important to read the right papers, to know what they are saying, but it is a mistake to rely on them. You can't always read in public like here."

"Where are you from?" she asked.

"Paraguay."

"What did you do there?"

"Dentist."

"You were a dentist? Why did you leave?"

Alberto put his hands together in front of his lips, then opened his hands in a gesture as if to say, 'who knows?'

"It is a dangerous place to live," he said finally.

"Do you have family there?"

"All. My wife. Three children. I could not bring them now, but I am sending money home. You like to see?" He pulled out his wallet and opened it to a photo carefully covered in plastic. Terry looked at a woman with dark hair piled above a round, pretty face.

Her fingernails were polished; gold glittered at her wrist. Her plump, graceful arms encircled three children: two boys, and a little girl in a frilly pink dress. The boys were smiling, one grinning broadly; the little girl was serious. She had Alberto's eyes. He ran his fingertip around the picture, then pointed to each and told Terry their names. She imagined him alone, holding the small, covered photo in both hands, lifting it to his lips as a priest would kiss a Bible.

"They're beautiful. All of them," she said.

"I miss them very much."

"Were you political there?" she asked.

"No."

She took a sip of coffee, feeling she had intruded.

"I need to learn good English so I can become a waiter. It is the most important thing for me—to get them out," Alberto said.

He had brought a small pad with him, and she watched his hands, deft and dark, as he wrote out simple verbs in neat handwriting. On his right hand, a small scar curved along the flesh between his thumb and his first finger. It looked like something from a childhood mishap, a soft, light crescent in his skin. She made a list of what she wanted to say: "I need a fork on table five." Alberto wrote: "*Yo neccessito un tenedor a la mesa cinquo, por favor.*"

On the way home, she strolled up Columbus Avenue. It was warm for January, and she bought a newspaper and sat down on a bench near the planetarium. She started to read an article on the front page, but after two paragraphs, she was confused. Funding for the Contras, Sandinistas, FMLN; the news was a mysterious conversation she was too late to catch up on. At least she knew that Paraguay was in South America, somewhere near Brazil. She knew that Central and South America were totally different, but they seemed tied together. Or maybe it was just her perspective. She thought of that poster of New York that showed Manhattan as the center of the earth: everything beyond New York was spread out and small, foreign countries, merely flattened mounds on the landscape. She pushed the paper into an overflowing garbage basket.

Down the block, next to the planetarium, a group of schoolchildren was getting off a bus. Each child paused before jumping off the last step; a curly-haired woman in a slicker held their arms as they hopped down. The children milled around on the cobbled sidewalk; the few who wore bright rubber boots marched fearlessly through the slush; others picked their way around the cobbled puddles. Her parents had brought her to the planetarium when she was small. She remembered thinking that the chairs were like church; when she leaned against the back, her knees didn't meet the edge and her feet stuck out. She had rubbed her hand back and forth against the upholstery nap, feeling the small resistance that could be pushed just so far before it bent the other way. And she remembered, so clearly, the deep, baritone voice of the man who explained the galaxies and the way the planets and stars were made. The lights went out, his voice boomed out of the ceiling above her, and somehow she was spinning back to the beginning of time, before dinosaurs even, and then—she fell asleep. It became a family joke, how much she'd looked forward to going, then fell asleep. She had begged her parents to take her back. She was sure she had missed something important, a kind of necessary secret, and when she fell asleep the second time, and woke to find her mother rubbing her arm and the yellow lights coming back up, she had cried so hard that her father had to carry her back to the car. Of course they thought she was crying because she had missed the lights, the stars, but what she couldn't explain was that she cried because, once again, she had missed the large voice that explained how everything worked. She sensed that in this unraveling of the earth's beginning there was a secret, some clue to looking forward and understanding what the future held. Her newspaper started to fly out of the garbage bin, and she stuffed it back down. Has she been asleep without knowing it? She had persisted and worked hard because it seemed that everything was possible, eventually she would make it. Had she missed what the voice might have said? She wrapped her coat around her and got up from the bench.

No one called about the part. Every morning, it was her first waking thought. Some days she tried to forget it; on others, she checked her phone machine every hour. She wished she had someone to talk to. She didn't tell anyone in her family because one person would surely tell another and she didn't want to raise their hopes. Karen was gone. She touched a photo crookedly tacked to her kitchen cupboard, a picture of her and Karen, their sophomore year at college. They had studied acting at Syracuse and moved to New York together. Karen was so much her physical opposite, blond and petite, that they rarely auditioned for the same parts. They both knew this was a factor in their long friendship. Last year, after a long streak without work, Karen had gotten a toothpaste commercial. Then one evening, when they were sitting at home, drinking a bottle of wine, Karen's agent called to say she was on the short list for a commercial for some kind of new sanitary napkin, something with wings. *With wings,* they had laughed hysterically, and in the midst of their laughter, Karen sat up very straight and looked at Terry. "I've spent ten years working at this and my career is going to consist of toothpaste and Kotex commercials?" Neither of them knew what to say. A few months later, Karen met a Venezuelan businessman at one of her waitressing jobs and she simply left—got married and moved to Caracas. She'd left Terry a long letter with a check written on her fiancé's account for an amount far exceeding several months' rent. Aside from the loss of her friendship, Karen's defection had set up a corrosive sense of doubt. Terry tapped the photo by its corner and spun it around on the tack. Roulette. This was all a crap shoot. She was almost glad to go to work that night.

After the shift, she and Sergio sat over a carafe of red wine and she told him about her audition.

"So the fact that I haven't heard from them is driving me crazy. Sometimes I think they don't want me. Sometimes I think they need to cast other people before they tell me yes, or maybe they have to see me read with someone. It could mean they're having production problems; it could mean they don't want me." She always circled back to this.

"Oh! A movie!" Sergio's hands fluttered around his mouth. "How long has it been since you read for the big man?"

"Three weeks."

"That is not long."

She knew he was right. She was too impatient. She wished she could think about something else.

"Where are you from, Sergio?"

"Peru."

"Why did you leave?"

"A queen like me?" Sergio laughed. "I would not be tolerated in the town I come from, and I tell you," Sergio leaned forward, confidential. "I always knew I would come to New York. Always," he patted her hand. "If you believe you are meant to be in the movies, then you will get your part." He poured her a glass of wine, "You should have your numbers done."

When Marie was satisfied with Terry, she let her work dinners, which was harder work, but better money. At night the back dining room looked wholly different: tiny lights on ficus trees placed strategically around the room reflected up into the large skylight like a thick net of stars. Spanish music played quietly in the background. She charmed a fresh audience of customers each night; some of them flirted with her, and she smiled lightly, promising them nothing without being too standoffish and jeopardizing her tip.

When Alberto was assigned to work with her, everything flowed more smoothly. Silent and efficient, he orbited her gracefully; he watched the tables without hovering, took care of things before she asked. He smelled of something soft and unfamiliar, not cologne, but soap maybe, sandalwood. She watched him from a distance as the shift slowed down. A dentist. Could his family imagine what his life was like? She imagined him sitting in his apartment at night, writing his letters home.

Sometimes she thought about him at night, before sleep. He had a wife, a whole family. *Stop thinking*, she told herself. It seemed she'd been telling herself this for weeks now, about every aspect of her life—stop thinking, don't imagine, don't want. "You're just lonely," she said out loud and it sounded melodramatic. "All you want is a distraction," she whispered to herself. She fell asleep and dreamed of visiting Alberto at his home in Paraguay. Everything was white. Stone white road leading to his house, white stucco walls. Lots of bright flowers. His wife was gracious, but she studied Terry silently; she knew that something had happened. Terry woke from her dream feeling guilty. Nothing's happened, she told herself. Nothing.

Several mornings a week she met Alberto in the sunny back room. He was always there first, shirt pressed, tie done up. She wrote out the sentences for what she needed to learn: "Table eight needs soup spoons. These are not the right glasses for red wine." Alberto took the piece of paper and wrote the sentences in Spanish underneath. His hands were long and slender; they didn't match the broad curves of his face.

"Does it take a lot of money to get them out?" she asked.

"There are other problems than money."

"Will you have trouble with papers, green cards?"

"Yes."

She picked at the edge of the paper he had written on.

"Nothing is safe. Even if you are very careful. No political. Fear, carefulness, these do not protect you in my country."

She looked at him for a long moment. She wanted to touch his hand, to run her finger along the soft crescent scar. She moved her hands in her lap. She wanted to say something comforting, to offer some small article of faith, but any sureness she might offer would be a platitude, and false.

"Has anything happened to people that you know—at home, I mean?"

"Yes."

One of the other waiters had heard her question and said something in Portuguese. Alberto shook his head.

"You should tell her about that. Learn those words," the waiter prompted.

"There are some things that should not be translated," Alberto said.

"What?" Terry asked.

"There are things I do not want the words for in any language." Alberto took his pad and closed it. "Time to go to work."

Lunch that day was hectic, but even in the rush, she checked her answering machine twice. She had the feeling that someone was trying to get in touch with her, but each time she called, her own voice answered. Maybe they're deciding now, she thought. Maybe they're choosing me this minute.

After the shift, Sergio made a hot meal for the staff. For the busboys, she guessed it was their biggest meal of the day. Sergio, because Marie decreed it, usually served a cheap cut of meat and some rice, as well as whatever vegetable soup was left over from lunch. Terry made herself salad. That afternoon, Marie noticed the dishwasher eating a cup of seafood chowder and she stormed into the kitchen to yell at Sergio who marched her right back out the swinging doors.

"One cup left! One cup! You want I should save it for dinner? It's for this little one here." Sergio loomed over the dishwasher and smoothed his hair like a woman soothing a small pet. "You will have no chef for dinner if you don't get off my back Marie!" Sergio's voice rose to a shriek and he swept into the kitchen. Marie hurried after him. Alberto looked up at Terry and smiled.

When she was done eating, Terry asked the bartender for a glass of red wine and sat down at a separate table to count her tips. Alberto sat at the end of a long table with the others. When he tipped back in his chair, his shirt pulled open at the collar and she saw the long scar, the soft skin like a crooked pink finger, running from the corner of his jaw, down the side of his neck. She felt her throat go tight, her fingers tremble. She closed her fingers around the stem of her glass. Alberto set the front feet of his chair back down on the ground and gently pulled his collar closed. He tightened his tie.

The next afternoon Terry walked into the restaurant and saw Marie sitting at a table with a man Terry didn't recognize. Terry waved, but Marie didn't acknowledge her. The bartender looked more surly than usual.

"Hey, Tom," she leaned over the bar, whispering, "what's up?"

"There's money missing from the lunch shift on Monday and Marie is pissed off. Everyone who worked that day has to take a lie detector test," he said.

Terry snorted. In back, no one was talking about it. Sergio kissed her on the cheek and asked her to write the specials on the board. Alberto walked over and touched her arm.

"You heard?"

"Tom told me," she said.

"This is trouble," Alberto said slowly. "Missing money is no good."

That night, a small sign posted in the kitchen listed the employees who would have to take a lie detector test. The list included everyone who worked on Monday. Juan studied it and made a disdainful spitting sound.

"Marie is a pig," he said. "All that *coca* and still so fat. Miss Piggy." Juan pressed his finger up against the bottom of his nose. Terry couldn't help but laugh.

When she arrived to set up for lunch the next day, Juan wasn't there. Friday lunch was always the busiest shift, and by twelve-thirty, everyone was frantic. Water glasses went unfilled, tables were left uncleared; even Alberto couldn't keep up. One customer stiffed her badly. Every time she skidded into the kitchen, she wished she could transform the dishwasher into a busboy.

After the shift, they all settled down to eat. Sergio had made a pot of stew, something to soothe them. The dishwasher started to tell a story, something about his mother, but he was speaking too quickly for Terry to follow. Sergio pinched his cheek. The bartender ran into the room.

"Immigration!"

Everyone jumped from his chair. Sergio ran for the kitchen, the others for the Columbus Avenue exit. Three men in suits ran into the room just as the last pant leg flickered out the door. They shoved past Terry, dodging the fallen chairs, running out into the street. Terry grabbed her purse and ran after them. Pushing through the heavy door, she heard a screech of brakes. The sharpness of the sound seemed to ruffle the awning above her head. She blinked in the sunlight. There was no trace of the waiters' black and whites, and for a moment she felt deserted. Then she saw a motionless car on the other side of the street. She felt a pulse in her throat; she tried to swallow, but couldn't. The light changed and a stream of cars blocked her view. A loud buzzing filled her head. The traffic kept her from getting across, and finally she waded out into it, stepping up onto the bumper of a gridlocked taxi. The driver appeared to be shouting, but she only saw his angry mouth; she couldn't hear him through the glass. On the other side of the street, she pushed through a small crowd. Alberto was lying by the curb, his compact body bent at an odd angle, his left leg flung out in a grotesque sideways kick.

She knelt beside him. His head was twisted to one side and blood seeped out of his mouth. His tie was still done up. His eyes, slightly open, showed only white. She heard herself yelling for a doctor, but her voice was being sucked back inside her, her words no louder than a whisper.

She felt someone behind her, hands on her shoulders, a beard by her ear.

"There's nothing to do." It was the bartender; his voice was quiet. He pulled her by the shoulders, led her out through the small crowd.

She couldn't go back into the restaurant; she started to walk up Columbus Avenue. Behind her, the sound of an ambulance sang *late, too late*, but the siren's increasing loudness seemed small, inconsequential.

She passed restaurants and bars, passed the street where the planetarium sat at the edge of Central Park, and she thought of her childhood desire for that all-knowing voice, her fear that she had missed something she needed to know. She remembered the afternoon when Alberto talked about getting his family out, how she'd been unable to offer him any reassurance; his life had seemed so small against everything he faced. And suddenly she felt an overwhelming sense of randomness, as if the invisible linkages of cause and effect seemed to float apart, dissipate, and she saw the people moving around her in the street, in the restaurants and cafés, were not protected, or overseen, but tenuously connected—unblessed, but also unfettered. And in the swirl of randomness, she felt an odd sense of lightness and clarity, as if in this vast disorder anything might be possible. Over the past weeks she had compared her difficulties with Alberto's, and had known that hers were trivial, but she saw it didn't matter; it was necessary to keep going. In the end it was like that movie with the false endings, or the undulations of a long, long story—everything depended on where you left off. She would keep waiting for the call, keep auditioning, and in the end, the story she would tell herself would be one that would reconcile her with her eventual success or failure. Everything around her stood out in high relief. She looked up at the high windows with their stone decorations on the buildings above her, the bare gray branches rising beyond the wall around the Park, and the dome of the planetarium, which held those bright calculations of light, a story of contraction and expansion, and the delicate projections of how the turning world had come to be.

Writing through the Night of the Tiananmen Square Massacre
William Pitt Root

1. Language that follows war like hyenas

I'm thinking of Tiananmen Square, of how awkward
Chinese can be on an English tongue, of the tanks,
warhorses of our age, bearing down on the brave who
stood their ground too long, who died under the treads,

their bodies, according to witnesses, popping like melons.
I'm thinking of the language that follows war like hyenas,
disposing of the dead, the mad cackling in the dark
as the powerful jaws of distortion do their work.

Because brothers, sisters, sons, daughters are translated
into "hooligans" for dreaming, as only hooligans can,
of justice without war, for speaking truth to power,
hundreds at the hands of thousands are dying tonight.

2. Strange music of war

And I'm thinking of the strange music of war:
The skittering clatter of irontracks on stone pavement,
ponderous, monstrous, with that awkward crab-like agility,
and the howitzer's whoosh and boom, the high shells

soundlessly arcing overhead whistling just before
it's all over for those who hear but cannot possibly
run far enough to avoid the firestorm and shrapnel.
And I'm thinking, almost with nostalgia,

of a time I never knew, when Roman horsemen could ride
certain of victory over any foot soldiers, all of them
now dust, the last breath of each so long mingled
with our air that every breath we take includes

molecules of theirs. The horsemen rode mounts trained
to dance to the strains of particular songs, lifting
their forelegs in chorus, prancing to this side,
then that—pride of the Roman legions they were,

anathema to their enemies. Except that these heathens
had heard of the dancing horses so often they spoke
of them by their campfires, sometimes to praise,
sometimes to curse, sometimes to joke about them,

relieving their fears with "what-ifs." Until one such
what-if did happen. As always, the Romans approached
riding in formation, shields raised, swords drawn,
approached at a trot—the better to chase down

hapless fools fleeing before them at their own pace,
lopping off heads from above and behind. When the ranks
parted before them, as always, like reeds in the wind,
how strange that must have been, the first startling sight

as bedraggled musicians began rising up before them,
lifting their horns and cymbals, rasping at strings,
beating on drums, catching just enough of that melody
configured in the warhorses' hearts to divide them

from the plans of their riders, to start them prancing
and keep them sidestepping while their startled riders
cried out commands the music countermanded. Disarray,
disarray—No longer a unified front, no longer the

shod lockstep propelling the wall of brazen shields on.
Gone the solar certainty blazing from visored eyes. Disarray!
Disarray! On boomed the drums, crudely makeshift; on
piped the flutes, frail against spears; on rang the singing

horns raised to the sky; and on danced the dancers
in brilliant regalia—as foot soldiers ran among them,
thrusting up spears, long swords, jabbing, hacking;
and then came the archers running up from behind:

thrum of the bowstrings echoing, echoing,
clanging of arrows on helmets, ringing of sword against
shield and bone as the horsemen lurched and the horsemen
pitched and the horses under them danced as they fell.

3. Mist swirling skyward

I write thinking of you, distant brothers and sisters;
I write even as soldiers of the 27th Army drag your bodies
—bodies they deny—to mass cremation. Bonfires, bone-fires
consuming your hopes and banners in a single flame,

peel flesh curling back like parchment from your hearts,
as heavy smoke, so richly laden, is mounting the Forbidden City....
How can leaders continue to lie, when our own stars
beam down the readable imagery of slaughter? How can they

not remember how long and far the irreversible innocence
of such ashes must drift? Yes, I'm writing through the night—
it's not my tongue that's force-fed flame to make it mute—
as your cells burn, your dream massacred.... Now I'm hearing

how fine spring rain washes your blood-gleam from pavingstones
politicians yesterday insisted your living presence "defiled";
I hear, too, how dawn sun draws up out of soul-stained stones
skeins of mist swirling skyward ghostly as snow geese.

4. A world free to change channels

Sisters of the song, brothers of the bone,
with our ideals jutting from your flesh before us,
jetting from your severed tongues, how could your names
ever again be strange as copper on our tongues?

And yet, one knows it will be so. Already tonight,
vexed fans of the Braves vs. Giants telecast
have been calling in, in droves, bitterly protesting
that their show has been pre-empted by your martyrdom.

So now we witness students, teachers, day-laborers, dreamers
signing **Freedom** to a world free to change channels;
they are raising an outcry so contagious that plain folks bearing
straw baskets of fishes or bread, fruits or flowers,

suddenly straighten backs bent by lifetimes of submission
to those moving only to the tunes of their own courts,
those bowing to one another, those who suck the juices,
spit out human rinds. Workers alert in the streets stood

firm before the first soldiers, petitioning mercy for you
as you pled Justice and Freedom for all. In my country,
such blood-born terms—richly abused, freely translated
into shameless greed and glib deceit—occasionally gag us.

Like apples publicly polished, privately poisoned. And yet
some fruits, first savored, may so transform inspired tongues
it's said they can sing old songs new—as when the long
downtrodden conspire with young dreamers, as when

the defenseless stand, arms akimbo, before trucks cunningly wedged
to block a tank's passage. As when you who are young, daring
to speak truth to old Father power, see power hesitate,
listening to his own old song played back in your new key.

My Boots: Notes on Quality and Craft
William Pitt Root

1.

I choose the poorest shop, one far from the zocalo
where tourists like myself spoil things
for people like me.

          For Los Indigenos
who come down every morning from the clouds
through heavy mist luminous along dirt paths
feeding backroads from the mountains,
walking the miles in from Zinicantan
and San Juan de Chamula with folded woven goods,
animalitos, twiggy bundles of firewood
to set up shop by the cathedral, for these
we are indispensible. Ooohing and aaaahing
we buy and buy, bracelets and blouses,
rugs and rebozos, chiclettas from the chiquitas.
Bargains for us are a living for them,
and trade is, as always, a fine excuse
to have a look at each other in the process.

2.

I bypass cobbler after cobbler,
peering in and inquiring about prices
while in truth I'm keeping an eye out
for signs of the kind of poverty
I mean to lighten with my needs.

At last on a northwest corner
far from the rattle and blast of traffic,
I enter a cubicle dark and bare
as a monk's cell. No TV, no radio,
unplastered adobe. Here a rack
of handhewn planks stands empty except
for one pair of well-worn sandals
and another of skinny cats—
        one black, one calico—,

neither much interested in a gringo
who carries his boots in a sack.

El viejo is blind in one moonpale eye,
just about as deaf as me, glancing up
from the bald tire he's carving a sole from,
squinting against the square of daylight
I've stepped in through. A small boy,
his grandson, indifferent as the cats,
spins a wooden top on the packed dirt
glancing sidelong to see if I watch.

3.

Six months later, back in the States
at a local mall in the Land of the Free
where I've hauled my boots in
to have the soles restitched: Must've
been some sorry-assed butcher
got the last laugh on you with these.

A fall and winter of the Eastern Seaboard's
acid rain and snow, and too much scuffling
on the sidewalks of Manhattan,
have chewed right through the cobbler's thread
and shrunk the leather just enough
to make repair here in Poughkeepsie
a major impossibility.

So I'll tell you what: I'm holding off until
I get into back country again, come summer,
when I'll find myself a shop far far
from malls and all their shining goods,
where a man with his grandson works on
through the years turning his eyes to moons,
a man who uses the hearing he's got left
listening to his grandson on the floor
singing snatches of tunes about revolution
and spinning his top in the packed dirt,
who keeps his one good eye on the stranger
who'll talk to the boy or not,
who'll spin that top with him or not.
And he will do the best job he knows how.

Domestic Affairs
William Pitt Root

So now we want out,
and no wonder.
News videos shock us
like slaps in the face.

We thought it was like
we thought it was—the
starving kids and mothers
withering like apples
blackened on a summer sill,
the twig-armed, stick-legged
robed ones, babes in arms,
wandering in from some desert
without enough saliva left
even to whisper for help.

We thought it was like
they said it was—the
bad guys big with guns
robbing the countryfolk
and burning the fields,
armored vehicles charging
into villages of mud and dung
firing bullets cruel as hail
into hopes and dreams still
clinging to these people
innocent and tough as nails.
Havoc, with a grinning face.

We thought we'd do our good
work and be gone before
they had our names. But no,
it was more intricate
than they had said,

more intimate by far
than we had known.

        I remember once in my late teens
        in San Francisco between terms
        I heard a woman scream from an alley
        by the bar I'd just rustled for 3
        illegal vodkas—they were good and I
        was brave with the magical potato,
        so I wandered to the rescue
        just in time to see a big guy
        smack her in the chops so hard
        her glasses landed at my feet.
        I'll never forget the red plastic
        frame-flash skittering toward me.
        Stalled just a second by my tardy
        sense of rude intrusion, I gawked
        then croaked, "Hey, lay off." Pretty,
        even messed up. So I thought as he
        smacked her again, not taking his eyes
        from me once as he did it. "Fuck off,
        kid, it's private." Her thick dark hair
        half hid her runny face and I could
        smell hot tears from where I stood,
        my sympathies impassioned. "Lay off,"
        I roared and charged into the darkness
        loaded with his fists, her purse, the
        cocked knees of both parties, until the alley
        pavement stopped my face. "Private,
        I said," he said. And arm in arm
        they left me there, to learn.

For Tim, without Whom
William Pitt Root

We first met at the backdoor when you knocked in the rain
looking for your high school friend since gone crazy,
the West Point washout who raced from Jesus and Mary
to Judaism then Viet Nam then came back with the pain

so common in those days, boasting of wasting kids
in one boozy breath, confessing he'd simply washed out
yet again in the next, sent home as a Section Eight
inveighing against the gooks, the niggers, and the yids

with the simple, disjunct insistence of the insane.
But he didn't come home that Sunday morning we waited
and chewed on Aquinas and Nietzsche and contemplated
each other in the gaps of our dialogue out of the rain.

Your impression, I gathered later, was that I was brooder
and dangerous, but capable of the occasional phrase;
mine was that you were a tough guy, amusing, enormous—
Irish as Paddies' own pig, and demonstrably cruder.

The years since then have rolled by in tides of wives,
our daughters washing up out of the surf like pearls
we've banked against emptiness in our scurrilous perilous
quests for respite, amid the riptides of our fluent lives.

The New World Gift
William Pitt Root

Mud to your familiar lovers,
cuppa java, Joe,
but after
our all-nighter
of mescal, spewing laughter,
you become the stern nun
friendly in your dark habit, serious
black mirror to the shapeless face
drawn up vaporous at dawn by the
bitter allure in your promise
of a better world to come.

                              Oh Mother Superior
of Grave Sobriety, how you shine
with your international spice!

Devil-may-care spelunker,
        keeper of such bad company,
how easily you go down
        into the open cup
of the gullet, alerting the long cave
        of the body
to sunrise, firing our dazed eyes
        with a light
to counter the cosmic dazzle.

Thank you, water's shadow-sister,
essence of meditative onyx,
rum's sober uncle.

                And isn't it also true
you once were a Zuni omen
for the milkbright, sky-eyed hordes,
of whom it was said
that they would signal their arrival
by holding out one hand full of the absence of gold
while the other balanced that prophetic cup
in which, henceforth, the world of old ways abruptly darkened?

Surprised by History
William Pitt Root

And just who is this witness so insatiably yawning,
this Cyclops whose black socket
once housed the hooded glare of a great star,
this blind Inspector General of bad faith

whose hope is sealed up black in a heart of adamant
while the twin lungs once inspired blow
immeasurably listless, thin wings flailing
blocked breast. Its stare is black as patience is

when blood rises to History's knees.
Black as the procession of figures
stunned into statistics while they
stagger across pages of unmarked snow.

Under the Influence of Celery
William Pitt Root

Snack-ravenous and sick of sweets, I come to you, at last,
at the bottom of the icebox,
nuzzled by a litter of spilled cherry tomatoes.

Bundle of ionic mothers—puzzled
and chilled by such unlikely progeny—,
how wisely my ten sandaled toes point you out
even as my unruly eyes explore smoked meats,
cheeses, and my conscience recites
its prim litany of carcinogens
I've loved all these years
bringing me to you just as I am—
a supplicant as naked in sandals
as the Sonoran sky is
    blue after rain,
kneeling till my knees ache
    in front of the open fridge
before the scales fall from my eyes
and I reach for you, fibrous and delicious.

And now I must apologize for such careless poetry.
I see you are not mothers.
               If anything
you are clustered sisters
whose presence evokes a Greek temple haunted
by sacred freshness.

You belong upright, like this, parallel and columnar,
green curls loosely dangling
while your very stillness penetrates
            to the heart of dance,
a frieze your vegetable scholars surely recognize.

I pull one of you free and immediately
relish the pale curve of
the long inner thigh made straight
by an irresistible pull from the sun,
           your verdant brilliance
drawn from terrestrial darkness by astral fire!

I think of my lover, visiting her sisters
in a place far from here,
then of my daughter, learning love this summer
in a place just as distant,
and I consider just how it is
we humans keep bringing such fire into our eyes
from the night of the loins and belly
despite the regular flights of eagle-eyed Doubt
and the canker it tends in the best-lit heart.

Seeing it all so clearly
under the influence
of celery,
I am uneasy.
                    How
can I ever
eat you, now that you are
lover, daughter,
and I a mere man standing naked,
dumbfounded, not a pretty sight
in the shambles of his kitchen
rummaging for a snack?

I eat you because
I am alive
and you
are to be known—not wasted
by wanton sentimentality stalling you
                         in the food chain,
preventing your transformation into consciousness.

I eat you because
as I love those closest to me
so I love you,
and I would have us all consumed by love.

I eat you because I am hungry
and you are food
and sometimes life is this good
and such is the poetry by which we become most ourselves.

Starblind

Richard Ryal

Crazed with knowledge of how tiny his telescope,
    how small his head, the astronomer
    torched his observatory, raised a flare,
          dimming the star specks
          around his planet.
Up and down are local gravitational concepts,
    he told his students, irrelevant terms
    beyond the pull of weightfulness,
          now he faced his flame
          with no navigational constants.
Wishing he could slip the earth's pull and slide
    into the width of space, he threw himself
    at the sky until he hurt too much
          to lift a finger or toe
          from the ground.
Firefighters mistook him for a vagrant
    spread back-down in mud on the crest
    of a twinkling hillside, face dancing
          with reflected fire
          at the fringe of darkness.
He told police the universe is above and below us,
    all its inhabitants travelers, he a lost comet,
    a fallen sky splinter, so nurses carried him
          to the Heavenly Body Home
          and made his nest on the ceiling.
Suspended in a net bed, he hangs his loosely curled fists
    over the floor tiles, his eyes reflect our galaxy
    as seen from a point in open space, a position
          his students try to compute
          by staring into his pupil-filled globes.
Nothing rouses the old man's response except
    a meteor chunk pressed to his palm
    which he clenches like a bird of prey
          and he utters *rrrrrlllllmmmmm,*
          a word we do not know.

"Cuttin' Up"
JOHN TOMS
(pastel on paper)

Drawing the Line
Lawson Fusao Inada

for Yosh Kuromiya

I.

Yosh is drawing the line.
It's a good line, on paper,
and a good morning
for just such an endeavor—

and the line seems to find
its own way, flowing
across the white expanse

like a dark, new river...

II.

Yes, Yosh is drawing the line.
And you might say he's simply
following his own nature—

he's always had a good eye,
a fine sense of perspective,
and a sure hand, a gift

for making things ring true,
and come clearer into view.

III.

So the line makes its way,
on paper, charting a clear
course like a signature,
starting from the left

and towards the bottom-end,
logically and gradually
and gracefully ascending

to the center where it takes
a sharp turn upward, straight
towards the top before it
finds itself leveling off

to the right again, descending
slightly for a while before
dropping straight down, coming
to a rest near the bottom,

bending, descending gradually
and gracefully as it began, but

at the other side of the space...

IV.

No sooner said than done.
Yosh relaxes for the moment,
blinks his eyes, realizing

his intensity of focus, almost
like prayer, a sunrise meditation

of deep and natural concentration.

V.

Ah, another beautiful morning!
Time to move on, see what the day
provides by way of promise...

And as for the drawing, well,
the line is drawn, on paper—

other dimensions can come later...

VI.

Yosh, although a young man—
a teenager—is naturally
calm and confident by nature.

Thus, when he draws a line,
it tends to stay drawn.
He'll make adjustments,
but doesn't make mistakes.

That's just the way he is—
trusting his own judgement
as a person, as an artist.

As a result, he is a most
trusted friend, judging
from the many friends who
count on him, rely on him,
respect what he has to say...

That's just the way he is—
"good-hearted," as they say:
"If you need a favor, ask
Yosh; he'll go out of his way..."

VII.

Still, though, "You've got to draw the line
somewhere"—and as the saying goes,

so goes Yosh, and his friends know
certain things not to ask of him.

What "everybody does" just may not go
with Yosh, the set of beliefs, the sense
of integrity, values, he got from his folks.

VIII.

As for this drawing in his sketchbook,
you might well ask: "What is it?"

As is, at this stage, it's just a line—
a line that goes sideways, up, over,
down, descending to the other margin.

Is it just a line? An abstract design?
Or might it stand for something?

At first glance, it looks to be a line
charting the progress of something
that goes along slowly, rising
a bit to indicate, oh, maybe a normal
growth rate or business-as-usual

when all of a sudden it jumps, reflecting
a decisive turn of events which lasts
a while before returning to resume

what might be assumed to be a more
regular course of activity concluding

at what may represent the present
on the journey from the then to the now...

That's what graphs show, the flow
of activity, the rise and fall of events
often out of our hands, so it can become
gratifying to simply resume the bottom-
line of normalcy again, starting over
at square one, back to the drawing-board...

That is, it could have been worse.
The line could have been broken, snapped,
or bottomed-out into nothing, going
nowhere fast like the slow and steady
line monitoring a silent patient...

Or, the line could have turned back
into itself into a dead-end maze,
a meaningless mass of angles and tangles...

Ah, but if you asked an observant child,
the answer might be: "Well, it just looks
like the bottom of my baby sister's mouth—
'cause when she smiles, she only has one tooth!"

And if you asked Yosh, he'd simply say,
in his modest way: "Oh, that's just Heart Mountain."

IX.

Maybe you had to be there.
For if you were, you would not only
not have to ask, but you would
appreciate the profile, the likeness

of what looms large in your life
and mind, as large as life staring
you in the face day by day by day

and so on into night, where it is so
implanted in your sight and mind
the unmistakable promontory protrudes,
a prominence in your mildest dreams,
and even when the dust billows, or clouds
cover it, blowing snow and sleet and rain,

you can't avoid it, you can count on it,
Heart Mountain, Heart Mountain
is still there. And you're here.

X.

Ah, but it is, after all,
just a mountain—one of many,
actually, in this region,
in this range, and if anything
distinguishes it, it's just
its individual shape and name.

And the fact that it stands
rising up out of the plains
so close you can touch it,
you can almost but not quite
get there on a Sunday picnic,
your voices echoing in the ever-
green forest on its slopes...

As it stands, it is a remote
monument to, a testament to
something that stands to be
respected from a distance,

accessible only in dreams,
those airy, carefree moments
before the truth comes crashing
home to your home in the camp...

XI.

Yosh can take you there, though,
by drawing the line, on paper.

And Yosh, with his own, given name,
is somewhat like the mountain—

an individual, certainly, but also
rather common to this region.

He's just so-and-so's kid,
or just another regular teenager
engaged in whatever it takes these days...

But this morning, it was different.
He was out there at the crack of dawn,
pacing around over by the fence,
blowing into his hands, rubbing
his hands, slapping, clapping
his hands together as if in preparation

to undertake something special
instead of doing the nothing he did—

that is, he just got to his knees
and knelt there, facing the mountain.

Knelt there. Knelt there. Is he praying?
But now he's writing. But writing what?

Then, as sunlight struck the mountain,
and the ordinary idle elder
and the regular bored child
approached Yosh, they could tell
from the size of the wide sketchpad
that he was *drawing*—but drawing
what? Well, that's obvious—but *what for*?

XII.

Seeing the drawing was its own reward.
Boy, look at that! He's got it *right*!
You've got to admire him for that!

And, boy, if you really look at it—
in this sunrise light, under this
wide, blue sky—why, it really *is*
a *beautiful sight*, that majestic
hunk of rock they call Heart Mountain!

And to top it off, this talented guy
sure accentuates the positive, because
he *didn't* include the *posts and wire*!

XIII.

Yosh, smiling, greeting, is striding
toward the barracks. There's a line
at the mess hall, a line at the toilets.

Better check in with the folks. Mom's
all right, but Dad's never adjusted.
I may or may not show him the drawing.

It depends. He likes me to stay active,
but this might be the wrong subject.
It might rub him wrong, get him
in a mountain-mood of reminiscing
about California, the mountains of home.

And, heck, those were just hills
by comparison, but they've taken on
size in his eyes; still, when I fill in
the shading, the forest, tonight, maybe
he can appreciate it for just what it is:

Heart Mountain, in Wyoming, a drawing
by his dutiful son here with the family
doing its duties—kitchen duty, latrine duty...

I'll do my duties; and I've got my own duty, my
right, to do what I can, to see this through...

XIV.

The sketchbook drops to the cot.
Brrr, better go get some coal.
It's the least I can do—not worth
much else, me, without a real line
of work. But this art might get me
someplace—maybe even a career
in here! Doing portraits of inmates!

But out there is *in here* too, related—
it's a matter of perspective, like lines
of lineage and-history, like the line
between me and the fencepost, between

me and the flagpole, between stars,
stripes, the searchlight, and the guy
on duty in the guardtower, maybe
like me, from California, looking
up at the airplane making a line
of sound in the sky, searching
for the right place in a time of peace...

Yes, if I had a big enough piece
of paper, I'd draw the line
tracing the way we came, smooth
as tracks clear back to California;

and in the other direction, the line
clean out to the city of Philadelphia
and the Liberty Bell ringing testimony
over Independence Hall and the framing
of the Constitution. Yes, it's there,
and I can see it, in the right frame of mind...

XV.

No, you have no right
to imprison my parents.

No, you have no right
to deny us our liberty.

Yes, I have my right
to stand for our justice.

Yes, I have my right
to stand for our freedom.

XVI.

And this is where Yosh
drew the line—

on paper, on the pages
of the Constitution.

XVII.

The rest is history.
Arrested, judged,
sentenced, imprisoned

for two years
for refusing
induction under

such conditions:
"As-long as my
family is in here..."

Eventually arrives
a few sentences
of Presidential

Pardon, period.
But history
doesn't rest,

as Yosh gives
testimony,
drawing the line,
on paper, again.

XVIII.

This time, though, he's a free man
with a free mind and a very clear
conscience, having come full circle
to this clear spring at Heart Mountain.

And Heart Mountain, of course,
is still there, timeless and ever-
changing in the seasons, the light,
standing, withstanding the test of time.

And this time Yosh is free to roam
his home range like an antelope,
circling the mountain, seeing all sides
with new visions, wide perspectives:

from here, it comes to a narrow peak;
from here, it presents the profile
of a cherished parent, strong, serene;
from here, yes, it could be a tooth;
and from anywhere, forever, a *heart*.

Yes, that's about the truth of it—
once a heart, always a heart—

a monumental testament under the sky.

This time, though, Yosh is strolling
over a freshly plowed and fenceless field
with that very same sketchbook, searching
through the decades to find that rightful
place in relation to the mountain, wanting
to show his wife where the drawing happened,

where that quiet young man sank to his knees
in reverence for the mountain, in silent
celebration for such a vision of beauty
that evoked such wonder, such a sunrise
of inspiration, wisdom, and compassion
that the line drew itself, making its way
with conviction in the direction it knew
to be right across the space, on paper,

and yes, yes, the heart, the eye, the mind
testify this-is *right, here*, Yosh, hold
up the drawing, behold the mountain, trust
the judgement upholding truth through time
as the man, the mountain, the profile make
a perfect fit in this right place and time
for Yosh to kneel again, feel again, raise
his radiant eyes in peace to face the radiant
mountain, *Heart* Mountain, *Heart* Mountain—
and begin, again, with confidence, to *draw the line*!

A Couple of Rogues
Latha Viswanathan

The idea came to Shankar while squatting in the outhouse. Being a creative sort, he understood the process and continued squatting long after it was necessary. It was a good ten minutes before the steps of the experiment lodged themselves firmly in his head. A methane gas plant at the village temple was not only innovative, it would solve all its current financial problems.

His wife Meenakshi stood before the tulasi, the sweet basil plant that occupied a prominent spot in the backyard. The cook handed him a second tumbler of coffee and Shankar gulped it down while he glanced hurriedly at the headlines of *The Hindu* before rushing for his bath. As he dipped and poured water over himself, he made a list of things he would need for a trial run. Drying himself, he carefully replaced the sacred thread around his neck. Hunching slightly, he peered into the mirror and applied *vibuthi*, holy ash, in three lines across the length of his forehead. He grabbed the cap of his toothpaste and smeared the edges with his wife's Vaseline. He pressed the sticky outline to the middle of his forehead. This he filled in with a bright red.

"I'm off to see Mani."

"What for?" she asked.

"It's all rather complicated. I don't have time to go into it now. We have to do something during the upcoming festival to collect funds, save the honor of the temple."

Meenakshi shook her head and muttered to herself. When he turned purposeful like this, she suspected something strange was cooking in his head. She wanted him to acquire dignity in old age: at least, she said, during the retirement years. He heard her curse the fate of her horoscope written sharply on her head. All those years in the city scrimping and saving, she complained, she just wanted some peace and quiet. "A little respect as one of the senior couples in the village. Is that too much to ask?" she said.

He locked his bicycle under the *neem* tree outside the courtyard. The temple elephant swayed, swinging its trunk this way and that before curling the tip around a bundle of grass, carrying it to the mouth. The trainer, Nayyar, stood there snorting snuff. "Is Mani in?"

Wiping his nostrils with the towel on his shoulder, the trainer pointed to the *sanctum sanctorium* inside. Shankar waited outside the closed doors, listening to the tinkling of the bell as the priest finished his morning rituals of cleaning and decorating the dancing idol. The heavy doors creaked open and Mani came out, smelling sour in spite of his recent bath, bulging breasts shining with sweat.

In his right hand, he held the customary plate of offering. Shankar reached out with his palms to shield the camphor's flame, taking back the warmth, fingertips to eyes. "How much?" he asked pointing to the slotted metal box, the *hundi*, where the worshippers dropped their offerings.

"About two thousand. What do you think?"

Shankar perked up. He outlined his plan of action. Mani's face crumpled. He became silent. "Trust me," assured Shankar. "The idea is solid. You'll accomplish everything—the grand show, the procession around the streets, an overflowing *hundi*, the advantage of electricity on a Sunday morning—they'll be suitably impressed."

In the past, Shankar's experiments had produced minor problems. Of course, these had eventually been ironed out. Money was scarce and the temple needed help. He remembered their conversation two years ago, when Mani had first approached him for advice. "Times are changing, Mani," Shankar had said. "You need to liven up things here like Madras. You need music, special effects, the temple's own stall selling flowers and coconuts." The priest's eyes had rounded, eyelids batting wildly.

"Can we do all that?"

"Leave it to me," Shankar had said, wearing an expression worthy of his title, ex-emeritus professor of electrical engineering, AC College of Technology, Madras. He had taken the money and purchased a second-hand cassette player from Ambika's Electronics in Palghat. Into the machine he had inserted a tape, fiddling with an extension cord, pushing the plug into a socket near the idol. Instantly, the place was transformed. Mani's mouse-like chanting was submerged with the dramatic beat of drums. The heavy walls vibrated with lively sound. People passing by had stopped in their tracks. A few went so far as to remove their footwear and go inside. The old woman who guarded slippers outside squatted firmly, planting a servile look in her eyes, motioning repeatedly to those peering curiously from the streets to come, visit inside.

The same day after sunset, the evening *puja* had drawn a big crowd. It was nobody's fault that the half-blind idiot Govindan had tripped the cord with his walking stick, shattering the drama of it all at the crucial moment, towards the end, as the little boys clanged the bells. Everyone noticed that Mani's voice squeaked more than before with the lack of background. Some of them opened their eyes, dropped folded palms and smiled. Still, it was nobody's fault that the only available socket was so close to where the faithful lined up.

Shankar's other invention was almost a success. The cracked sandstone *lingam* beside the idol was replaced with a shiny, dark phallus in bronze. The design was ingenious, Mani had had to admit. The top part sat on grooves, fitting neatly onto the bottom half. The practically invisible hole on top and the fine chicken wire sieve around the bottom drained and collected the liquids underneath: milk, buttermilk, honey and *ghee* that Mani poured daily on the *lingam*. The temple had saved a bundle by recycling holy liquids.

For two blissful weeks, things went smoothly. After that, the rats had come. They chewed through the chicken wire at night. Mani discovered another flaw. The *tulasi* leaves and flower petals choked the fragile filter, making liquids leak out, mapping the stone steps, creating havoc on the floor below where sticky footprints were soon covered with ants.

Shankar thought his affinity with the elephant was a definite asset to his new plan. When he came by with his everyday offering of two rather over-ripe bananas, the elephant dropped the palm frond, assuming a greeting stance. It probed the man's armpits and crotch, savoring the familiar smell. Having made contact, it let out a rumble, irresolutely swinging the trunk, then curling, preparing to trumpet again. This bumptious twiddling went on and on till Shankar produced the bananas. Using the tip of the snout as a scoop, the elephant lifted the fruits efficiently. By the time Shankar left, the animal was busy scratching its rump, rubbing against the trunk of the nearest breadfruit tree with half-closed eyes.

This being October, a period of *musth*, the elephant was slightly in rut. Hurling balls of shit at the trainer, it had gathered the chains and fetters, piling them into a heap, and gone on strike. Nayyar said it refused to obey commands, ramming tusks into the trunk of the breadfruit tree, rolling crazy eyes. First thing in the morning the animal greeted him by tossing a breadfruit. Nayyar had been caught off-guard: his attempt to duck the flying fruit had failed. "Randy bastard," he had yelled, clutching his cheek now turning purplish black.

Shankar had just returned to the temple from the neighboring village where he had gone to visit an old friend. Seeing him, the trainer wrung his hands, saying, "I think we need the medicine. What do you think?" Shankar said to follow him.

He explained to Meenakshi that he was in a rush.

She ignored him and asked, "What happened to you?" pointing to Nayyar's face.

"He threw a breadfruit at me," mumbled the man, stroking the sore spot.

"In musth again? That elephant is a rogue, that's what." She scolded as if the man was responsible for the condition, Shankar thought. She disapproved of the androgen tablets that were passed on to the trainer. "Tampering with nature, that's what it was." Like most others in the village, Shankar realized, she believed seminal fluid to be vital for health. "Sacrilege," she said. "Whoever heard of stuffing a Siva temple elephant with hormones? I want no part of the plan." Watching Nayyar flinch as he tried to speak, she went inside, grumbling to herself. "May Siva forgive you your sins," she said to Shankar as he folded the envelope. She handed Mani two extra bananas, being the good Hindu woman she was. Perhaps she believed that would atone for his chemical indiscretion, Shankar thought.

Her contribution to the elephant's well-being was an herbal concoction she made with other women. Shankar watched as they mixed oils of garlic, camphor and gardenia. She instructed Nayyar to dilute and pour the paste; it was a natural insect repellent and antiseptic for sensitive skin. She said herbal medicine was better; one knew what went into such things. "Mysterious hormones that one can't decipher, that's something else," she muttered. Looking at her face, catching the fleeting scorn, Shankar could match the words to her thoughts. What to do? Does a husband listen to a wife? Men were stubborn goats. She had given up long ago. Shankar tried to distract and calm. He described the photograph of a wonderful lamp he had seen in his friend's house.

"An American magazine," he enthused, hoping to impress. She snorted in reply.

Mani and Shankar came out of the temple with the feeling that all sorts of things were possible. The plan was airtight. The elephant stood on pillar legs while Nayyar filed his nails. The animal was the color of stone, whooshing urine by the gallon. Testing the wind with his single finger, the elephant picked up the towel on Nayyar's shoulder and laid it on a branch. "Fetch that back," scolded the trainer. The two watching men suppressed a smile.

The carbon steel drums were delivered the following week. Nayyar wasn't sure that four were enough. The animal defecated twenty times a day. The quantity was enormous. He got hold of urchin boys who shoveled the mounds all day long. "Make sure they leave space on top," warned Shankar, covering half his face with a towel, holding his breath as he supervised. He inspected the funnel lids that went on top. "The idea is similar to a compost heap," he explained to Mani as the rotund man watched. The sagging drums were left to dry in the sun. Being a stickler for hygiene, the priest said he resented the swarms of flies in the compound.

Back at the house, Meenakshi had heard the news. "This fascination with elephant dung," she asked, "who are you trying to impress?" Standing before him, she slapped her forehead. "Because of you, I can't step out of the house. They're laughing. They think you're a lunatic," she gestured with her hands.

"Who's laughing?" he thundered and proceeded to the front door. He unlocked the bolt and looked to left and right. "I don't see anyone. You're becoming neurotic, that's what. I'll send for the taxi tomorrow. Why not go visit your grandchildren in Madras?" Meenakshi stopped her protests immediately.

A dreamy look settled in her eyes. "Send for the taxi. You do that," she agreed. " I'll leave instructions with the cook."

He had not expected her to agree to leaving so quickly. It was just fine with him, he consoled himself. He could carry out his plan without interference from a nagging wife. If Meenakshi wasn't around, he thought, he'd convert the bore-well motor to a generator and drive the turbine. She fussed about ample water for her bath, washing her hair daily, as if anyone cared about an old woman's gray hair.

A moment of contentment came over him after dinner though he'd cursed earlier when the power went off. The hissing gas lamp had a lulling effect; his eyes grew accustomed to the softer light. He dozed on and off sitting in his easy chair. He woke up scratching, devoured by mosquitoes that attacked with renewed energy realizing there was no ceiling fan. The power cuts were insane, he had to agree with his wife. She was sitting by the threshold, waving a gaudy Japanese-style plastic fan. "It will be lonely without you," he mumbled grudgingly, eagerly searching for a sign. She continued fanning herself, first the face, then her neck which she extended by lifting her chin.

"You won't even know I'm gone; I see no difference whether I'm here or there," she said and sighed. Shankar knew his sixtieth birthday was coming up, a time to renew wedding vows. She had hinted about coral beads for a chain around the neck.

The tablets had taken effect, and the elephant's behavior turned tractable again. The animal's dark shape and loose skin cloaked his manliness, the belly sagging again as he gobbled up everything in sight. Shankar noticed he was wallowing in mud, bathing with dust. The mosquitoes and fleas were numerous after the rains.

On the day of the festival, Shankar saw that Meenakshi and the other women sat surrounded by baskets of flowers. They unwound bundles of banana fiber casting with deft fingers, knotting together lotus petals, roses and other flowers. Young girls sat to one side jabbing stems of jasmine with needles and stringing them with twine. The scent of roasting vermicelli swam through the air. Street vendors flaunted a strange combination of knick-knacks: iridescent bangles, khaki mountains of henna, cone-shaped packets of peanuts wrapped in childish handwriting that outlined steps to theorems from last year's class, crepe paper elephant kites with streaming snout tails that waved when the wind picked up and wobbly spools of kite-thread reinforced with glass dust.

He caught up with Nayyar and the elephant as they walked towards the pond. The elephant bathed for an hour. The trainer scrubbed the tusk, the smoothened worn right one (the elephant was right-handed) with a clump of coconut fiber, murmuring endearments all the time. Drops of water clung to the stiff bristles of the animal's chin. He rested his trunk on the upturned sharp left tusk, relishing every minute of the ritual, knowing it was a time for man and elephant to bond.

Walking back to the temple, Shankar noticed that the old woman guarding slippers outside sat by the pavement with glazed eyes. Her pierced earlobes drooped dramatically, grazing shoulders, stretched with decades of supporting chunky weights. The same fate seemed to have overtaken her breasts, which curtained her navel as she squatted on the mud. Her concave stomach, trained to fill easily with steaming tumblers of tea, rumbled in protest for a bit of rice. Her grandchild had made a basket of burrs. This she filled with bruised flowers which Meenakshi and the other women chucked out. Oblivious to the threads of snot that streamed down her childish face, she offered the container to her grandmother.

Later in the morning, crowds began to arrive. Shankar lifted the end of the PVC pipe snaking out of the drum. His nose twitched in anticipation, and he took a deep breath. He felt like the captain of a relay race. He plugged the open end to the valve of the gas cylinder. This, in turn, was connected to the makeshift boiler and gas burner. A gleaming brass vessel normally used for storing water had been loaned from the temple kitchen. The priest and the cook had objected to the use of the kitchen vessel, but it wasn't as if this was cow dung. He pacified them by camouflaging the vessel with a coating of mud.

Shankar waited impatiently as the pressure built up, planting piercing eyes on the turbine and generator. It was only a matter of minutes before the leads sizzled to life. The filaments inside the *lingam* gave off a steady warmth. The turbine blades revolved, the generator roared, and the crowd watched as the music turned deafening, Mani chanting at a high pitch. Shankar took off his glasses and wiped his face with his sleeve. The crowd stilled their shuffling feet. The wax coating on the *lingam* liquefied; the phallus responded with grief. The faithful watched the liquid trickle down, slapped their cheeks gently with palms in penance, for who understands the ways of Siva's wisdom. They were mere mortals, small creatures in the end.

Catching Meenakshi's face, Shankar nodded conspiratorially. He thought she slapped her cheeks harder. How many more births? her face read. Will the cycle never end? What kind of destiny was this that had made her marry a clown?

This elephant is going to be a star, Shankar thought. Meenakshi had lovingly patched the small tears in his shiny clothes. The mended brocade sheet looked majestic on his back. Leather harnesses of bells were wrapped around the legs, a useful warning for fools like Govindan. A velvet cape with scattered copper domes encircled the forehead. Nayyar tied a necklace of satin red rope with a big bell pendant around the neck. Pompoms made from yak hair bobbed up and down. The elephant's leafy ears waved in and out, driving away those pesky flies.

Nayyar's sons had assignments. The trainer was excited, a big day for man, sons and elephant. The older boy looked clearly bored; elephant duty was not on his mind. All those girls on the street below, a fine time to be pushing and shoving, smiling back at pretend severe looks in their eyes. Why did the brat grin and sway. Adolescent exaggeration, Shankar surmised. The boy's noisy friends whistled and watched. He went up to them, suggesting decorum, the procession was about to begin, couldn't they see that? They said they felt sorry for the elephant, pestered with all those clothes and accessories—not to worry, they had fixed that. They laughed raucously and left, scattering in different directions. Shankar's experienced nose detected toddy breath. Had Nayyar's son imbibed? He saw that the elephant had stopped reaching out with his trunk, was standing unnaturally still. He recalled that the animal loved sweet, smelly wine.

Surrounded by her friends, Meenakshi was chattering, looking a little in *musth* herself. Shankar winked at her and grinned as she blushed. He knew that look. She'd do more than talk about coral beads tonight. Shankar and the elephant ambled out of the temple, he with a smug look about the eyes, while the giant swaying his tender arm, a silly dolphin smile around the mouth. He heard the priest's voice, shrilly with delight, the trainer inhaling loudly, lungs coated with a film of snuff.

Nayyar's older son held the dancing idol on the wobbling back, the younger boy sat fanning the holy face with peacock fans. The trainer occasionally opened and closed a silk parasol trimmed with glittering thread. The priest and his assistants chanted in front. Approaching the fancy corner house, Nayyar commanded the elephant to halt. The family promised a large donation, Mani had been notified.

The camphor was lit and a plate was prepared with coconut and flowers, a return offering to the generous man and lady of the house. Shankar saw the elephant shift his weight wildly as if a maddening itch spread between the legs. No, he thought, the animal seemed to be contemplating the pillars in front of the house. Yes, the columns possibly reminded him of tree trunks. The animal turned around; the crowd screamed. The owner of the house and his wife gasped; the elephant reached out to grab. It was a while before he let the pillar go, heeding Nayyar's gentle tongue. Then the animal lay his snout on his tusks, becoming very still, preparing for a nap.

After an hour of waiting, the crowd grew restless. The idol was removed, and Nayyar and his sons dismounted in disgust. The elephant, statue-like, refused to react. Mani gesticulated and yelled hysterically at Nayyar. People were leaving. What about the coins and notes in his slotted box? The sleepy elephant picked up the priest deftly and deposited him on the roof of the house. The remaining children watched in awe. Mani grabbed the weather vane, and the circling bird squeaked in response. Shankar felt deeply for his friend. The priest's expression was variegated: the shock of the height, the feel of elephant skin, the sharp metal wing in his hand. Mani almost fainted, his towel slipping, the two mounds on his chest pointing towards the sky. Walking women stopped and laughed.

For Shankar the drama exploded into the night. The suspense of Meenakshi's pinched face, the silent treatment in bed. He kissed her fingers, promising to make up for the honeymoon they'd never had. He stuck his nose in her hair, saying softly, "Did you wash it again tonight?" She turned around innocently, targeting a fast knee, ripping his lust. No sorry, did it hurt, not a trace of regret. Acknowledging herself, she spilled the shame, the fate of being a coot's wife. Fooling around with shit drums, lecherous elephants, snuff-snorting types, a couple of rogues, she wailed, mourning with red eyes. Her fingers clasped and tugged the corner of his pillow. Who was this—his thumb-sucking grandson or his wife? She moved nearer, anticipating the contour of his body, this woman of mercury, his wife. No experiments, he swore, not outside the house.

"We never do anything together," Meenakshi said, "What about Sanskrit lessons?" Now that life here was organized, he thought, she worried about the next.

"Yes," he managed in a muffled tone, "arrange for anything dignified."

Mani worked alone, squeaking for hours, dissipating fat. "Poor man," Meenakshi said, "save the bananas for him."

Shankar noticed that the beggar woman in front of the temple lost her servile look. "No one came anymore, the temple was ordinary," she said. She was thinking of leaving; this village was a dead loss.

Meenakshi made him dizzy, folding the newspaper, massing magazines, fattening cushions on the divan, straightening the slant of his calendar on the wall. She snarled a command at the cook who stood staring out the window with idiot eyes. Shankar saw that she had combed out the snarls and piled her freshly washed hair. A few tendrils had dodged the pins, tumbling about on the nape of her neck. "I've asked for the jeweler to come in the afternoon," she said. "It's childish to procrastinate in our stage of life." He turned smoothly, detour on his tongue.

"Do you remember the light for the bedroom I talked about?" She played on, pretending to be deaf.

"Mani will be here any minute," she said, handing him the fruit. He looked up and shook his fist, a banana drill, piercing the sky.

The priest, his swelling chest hidden seductively under a honeycombed cotton towel, instructed in a monotone. Shankar tried hard to listen. He even picked up a pencil and followed the lines. Between the verses of the Geeta, he drafted a plan. He designed an American light for the bedroom, recalling details of the picture in his mind. When he had told Meenakshi about lights in America that turned on and off when someone clapped, she had dismissed it as foolish, irrelevant for their life. "We don't have to clap—just blink and the lights go off. Perhaps America is a big country, they need all that noise. Forget about lights with ears, why not design lights that shine?"

Always the smart one, not easily impressed. What to do? Does a wife listen to a husband? Women were silly sparrows. He had given up long ago. He had hoped that she would acquire some kindness, at least during this time. A little kindness, some love, was that too much to ask? "Would a sane woman go around clapping in the dark?" she had said. "Stark raving mad. Most women marry men. Only I married a fool." He looked at her and watched her snort.

Kneading his stomach, Shankar got up and walked. Life was impossible inside, better lived in the outhouse.

"Tye of Passion"
JOHN TOMS
(pastel on paper)

The Solitary Reaper: Themes and Variations
Jeffrey C. Robinson

"The Solitary Reaper" by William Wordsworth

Yon solitary Highland Lass!
Behold her, single in the field,
Reaping and singing by herself;
Stop here, or gently pass!
Alone she cuts and binds the grain,
And sings a melancholy strain;
O listen! for the Vale profound
Is overflowing with the sound.

No Nightingale did ever chaunt
More welcome notes to weary bands
Of travellers in some shady haunt,
Among Arabian sands:
A voice so thrilling ne'er was heard
In spring-time from the Cuckoo-bird,
Breaking the silence of the seas
Among the farthest Hebrides.

Will no one tell me what she sings?—
Perhaps the plaintive numbers flow
For old, unhappy, far-off things,
And battles long ago:
Or is it some more humble lay,
Familiar matter of today?
Some natural sorrow, loss, or pain,
That has been, and may be again?

Whate'er the theme, the Maiden sang
As if her song could have no ending;
I saw her singing at her work,
And o'er the sickle bending;—
I listen'd, motionless and still;*
And, as I mounted up the hill,
The music in my heart I bore,
Long after it was heard no more.

*till I had my fill (1807)

Preface
Jeffrey C. Robinson

William Wordsworth's "The Solitary Reaper," first published in 1807, has become a lyric monument. With chiseled tetrameter quatrains and couplets and with its perfectly rehearsed stanzas, it apparently fulfills all expectations, including a temporal drama of completion: the present-tense urgency giving way to a ripened recollection. The autumnal setting and activity of the reaper, her singing at once welcoming, comforting, and exciting, has its analogue in the fulfilling naturalness of the speaker's path of thought which surpasses the crisis of arrest, thrill, and curiosity with an achieved spiritual contentment.

But moral choices trap the reader of this poem. One either rejects the poem outright for its masculinist aesthetic in which beauty "mounts" upon the body and subjectivity of the female reaper, or one willingly and knowingly denies that in order to engage the beauty of the poem as a "work of art" and its representation of the male speaker's imaginative play. I cannot go all the way with either of these two responses. I would rather begin at the point of this impasse and think, with the Frankfurt School, that there exists an aesthetics of critical consciousness acknowledging one's situatedness within a system of the beautiful (and therefore celebrating the beautiful itself) shaped, nonetheless, by a deficit in its commitment to the representation of otherness.

But this is not enough. "The Solitary Reaper" contains within it the unrealized possibilities for undoing or transforming its limiting features. I have written this suite of poems to follow the lines of energy, sympathy, love, and vision latent or subdued in the original, to hear from the Reaper herself, to hear the dissonances between reaper and speaker as well as their harmonies, to recover the elements of play in language intimated in the songs of nightingale and cuckoo (acknowledged in my poems through quotation from other poets), and to erode the solitary, singular, monumental character of Wordsworth's poem (re-interpreting the idea of the eternal as the eternally recurring) into a river of poems, each one of which the original has sparked in a unique occasion.

1.

"some one intently passing through a world" "arrested by the momentary nature of things within an unfathomable 'order.'" (Cid Corman on Basho)

cosmos a cup
filling   overflowing   into   order
a depth of song in an iron time
the empty space

meter and rhyme the cup of that day
breaking the dark, intimate flow of
possible pain   the bending
female burden
order of birds and tales
water Northern geographies

arrested, I take my fill of oppression's
thrill-
          ing   song
her body closed and still in
hunger of rhyme

2.

She: single in her field
He: composes her by field
Much arises between them
No hierarchies, nothing suppressed
What's not known is not known
What's not heard isn't known
but images gather like swallows
          before passing
There are complexities, contradictions:
Fruit from the singing ground
He gathers her-gathering amidst stars.

*   *   *   *

3.

she, bent o'er
he, erect and mounting
draw your own conclusions

and I?

4.

Why do distant objects please? and what
Jewish melody Hebrew syllables Gematria
layers of history into collective field
do my eyes and ears cull

I am new here
some doubt keeps me wondering past
Wordsworth's fear of French invasions
his sucking up to nobles
condescension to Scots
maravigliando
substance of distance:
Kaddish of Spring?

*   *   *   *

5.

alone
Eurydice was "a root
                        self-rooted"
while Orpheus
        berating his desire…
she rages and cuts him
        bending   smiling

6.

"Passed by a Female
who was   reaping
                        alone,
she sung in Erse
as she bended o'er
                        her sickle,
the sweetest   human   voice
            I   ever   heard.

Her strains were tenderly
melancholy
& felt delicious
long after they
were   heard
no more."

"A beautiful sentence," said Wordsworth, about Thomas Wilkinson's
Tour in the British Mountains, read by the poet in manuscript on
or before his own 1803 tour of Scotland. When he journeyed to
Scotland in 1787, Wilkinson, according to DeQuincey, "a sort of
pet with Wordsworth," would often
"try their sickles,
and reap
and talk
with them."
William and Dorothy
stayed away
from sickles.   The poet
held back   viewing
the curve of the instrument
like the reaper's body bending,
"feet and head
coming
together
in life's pilgrimage."

7.

Poem overflows:
my faith.
Poem is "house
of the axe of lightening"—
oblong constraint
like a coffin, with voice unheard but
rolling towards me from the Vale's far end.
Honor boundaries of silence and speech.
Bouquet of whites and purples:
back bent and grime
at full risk to arrange
into the beautiful.

8.

Here, in this endless field
I sense a cold attention
Grain cuts me
He mouths something to someone else
        someone vague
But I am the "else," not his archetype
my words, nonetheless, tragically his—
he trying to keep them turbid and sweet

Oh God, before your mouth and face
I will gather my grain
I work you, I dirty you
in order that I may love.

9.

It's you,
        not the reaper,
                I call
over a Vale
           of bedded embers
off the road of breath
sickle in dry heat
Sufi cuckoo far-off
              I look
back:
        reapers in flight

I far from Grasmere
am home
You absorbed in a burning
field of diaspora

10.

from the milk of Theocritus
he composes, calls, culls me:
a Highland L-Ass.
Nightingales, seabirds
over wild seas, cuckoos,
play *La Creation du Monde*

Sweeter to walk back
from sleep to love.

11.

Scotland cutting down
Ellen Irwin, Bruce, Gordon:
killing field from passion
madness
      heartbreak
           beguiling the day
sacred dewy ground of blood
suite of memorials
ward off defacement
here lies....here lies...

"the formation of myths from words":
reaping-and-singing:
myth of labor and art
melting together, a
ringing-and-seaping
eternalizing labor as beautiful
So,
before oblivion seeps through
true labor,
sow the words into
unfamiliar
      hybrids
         of praise

12.

Reaper/Persephone

I.

screaming
        carried off
she had wandered
a flower of herself
alone to blue narcissus
Hades the jealous poet mounted

O Queen of cut and bound
blistered fingers
no greeny flowers returning

Zeus plots with Hades
no pomegranates   no song

II.

pomegranate   narcissus
analogues of solitude
lips unable to close:
poppy

III.

Mythology says I'm
insatiable in bed   yet
as Kore a virgin
as Queen of the Dead
gracious and merciful
my name means "she who
brings destruction"
my Latin name "the fearful one"

He stares at me
witch
houseless in
fear and rage

Vale of that which
is not reduced to ashes:
asphodel food for ghosts
my sisters and brothers

13.

    a   cave   of   emeralds
                             cocked
over her bent frame
song comes
              akin to sky
her miseries   my fears
walk on rutted roads
Je suis un autre.

mute   watching   you
a full half-hour
swamped in your oblivion
until this moment

now in two hundred years
your throat and mine
                  open
hand in hand

Sources in Poems

5. Rilke
6. Wordsworth (the final quote)
7. Salvador Espriu
8. American Indian (adaptation)
11. Michel Leiri

Suzannah, My Dear
Lisa Russ Spaar

Above the shrubs strung
with dew-stung hammocks of spider webs,
a flock of unexpected starlings
is building its aerial temple, dismantling
the sexual magnolia with a redneck aria.
Sun and moon stand off, two blooms,
one an upstart, pressing,
pressing, and one fading.
On such a morning, you came, songbird,
implausible gift; it was October then,
too, and you were crowning
to this music: Trane blowing
to words Monk insisted into song, *Ruby,*
my dear—Your face was red
and screwed with singing what you knew
of heaven, or with what you'd suddenly
discovered. Now we're on the road,
you're five, and lances of light
are cascading down the windshield
that flashes with passing, orange Bluebird buses
and the bloodrust snow of the year's confetti;
you are lounging, legs crossed,
chatting and humming into the high heel of a red,
dress-up shoe as though it were a telephone,
glancing up, now and then, at the leaves' descent,
lilting then descending in all those repeated
minor seconds, and I hear you saying, "Mama, you know,
when the world is changing,
like this,
you can really see it."

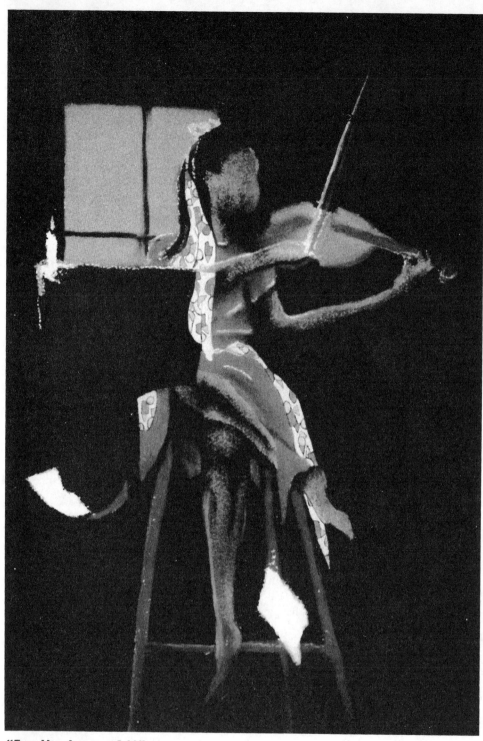

"For the Love of It"
JOHN TOMS
(pastel on paper)

Fugue
Carolyn Beard Whitlow

can see but not read
can read but not think
can think but not speak
the spoken unheard
the unheard written:

I scrub my hair with a floor brush,
dustmop my mouth, broomsweep my crotch,
womb inside a body pressed
to service like a dress worn thin—
sit by the window, naked
panes before me, write
archival footage, linger
over the page longingly, words
languid, grounded suspension of disbelief—
my ears stoop to listen,
emotions exposed like genitals
flashed, covered, flashed, neon
darkness, staccato light pulse
failed, envelope stuffed with male,
plain-cover rejections hand-stamped, post-
marked, my mind giftboxed, tonguetied, bowed
under, avalanched, buried
by thoughts unasked, unowned, not my own,
here and there a button pressed,
thoughts contained, words out on parole,
distrust a trust I must keep—
l-e-t-t-e-r-w-o-r-d-s whisper, sibilant,
labial voices in fugue, fuse, ignite
the darkening bloused within me
and I behind the blind do see
the difference between the poems
that live, those lines that
survive, these letters hung
on the lifeline,
d(r)ying.

Positions
Carolyn Beard Whitlow

1

This is a day of impositions.

2

Held now by chains of forgetfulness,
Unopened gates, the inner sanctum
Still, subliminal, labyrinthine,
My limber fingers tiptoe
Past Pandora's sealed box.

3

Your back a blackboard,
Fingers of soap—
This is a day of impositions:
My inner sanctum still,
Your lips, hands,
My many mounds—
My mind enters my womb,
Dives down down
To the bottomfilled depth,
Subliminal, labyrinthine.

4

Held now by chains of fullness,
This is a day of impositions.
You turn me
Like an egg over soft,
Beat my drum slowly,
Drum song dance
Tongue talking:
Tautness reverberates, cymbals resound,
Pandora's unsealed box.

5

This is a day of positions.
I give you my body
—a gift—
Legs wrapped round your back
Like ribbons,
Feet tied in a bow.

6

Pandora's sanctum unsealed,
Subliminal, labyrinthine,
Unstill, open—
My hips become peasant,
Calves and beeves,
My mind before me a melon,
Seed after seed after seed.

The Meaning of Romance
Kate Lynn Hibbard

It could have been any airport restroom in any city,
the yellow triangular "Caution: Wet Floor" sign
guarding the curved entrance without a door.

There we are, two grown women with carry-on
luggage, crammed into the last stall
in the ladies' room on Concourse B, lovers

kissing goodbye. We kiss to the sounds
of women sitting down with a sigh after holding
their pee for three hours on a crowded flight,

the weary tones of mothers telling their children
to use soap dispensers they can barely
reach, and "honey don't touch anything in here,

it's dirty." We kiss and listen to the cleaning woman
snap her gum and banter on the two-way radio,
making plans for the weekend while wiping

soap scum and hair from the sinks. We clutch
each other and my lover peers at me through smoky
aviator glasses she wears indoors to look mysterious.

She tells me she'll miss me. I think of Bergman
leaving Bogart in Casablanca, wonder how things
might have gone for them without the crutch

of backlit romance, no trenchcoats with the collars
turned up, no light planes whirring on a foggy runway.
I stumble out first, blink my eyes at a young woman

who stands at the sink repairing her hairdo.
She pulls a strand straight out from her scalp,
sprays mousse from a large can, and the air fills

with sticky drops that smell like piña colada.
Her puzzled eyes meet mine in the mirror,
brows furrowed in what could be a glare

but I choose to receive as benediction. And my lover
flushes the toilet before leaving the stall,
as if we had something to hide. Is this the beginning

of a beautiful friendship, confronting desire
in a little room designed to eliminate
refuse, what extravagance the body needs to release?

Gavacho
Bobby Byrd

Lying on another man's shoulder,
the man in the red hat has his hand inside my pants.
He is feeling my penis.
Limp thing.
His family doesn't seem to mind.
We are in Juárez which is no longer the other side.
The grandmother is serving albondigas,
there's some
asparagus and a potato casserole.
The brother who is a writer is
at the other table with his friends.
They are holding hands and having a seance.
They want to speak with Emilio Zapata.
They want to speak with Pancho Villa.
Nothing happens. It never does.
Trash is on the floor.
I start cleaning it up.
I enjoy the feel of a broom in my hands.

Dream of a Sunday Afternoon in La Alameda Central
Bobby Byrd

Blas, your favorite waiter,
the handsome Indian looking man
with the broad smile,
serves you a cappuccino
at El Trevi,
a good but inexpensive restaurant

    which today
   seems
to be a pretty good answer

to the question of existence,
especially if you, like me
(a gringo, an improvisational wanderer
of Mexico City streets),
have completed the obligatory
Sunday evening, promenade
back and forth
through the crowded walks
and tall dark trees
of La Alameda Central.

        If so,
you've seen and meditated on
the man with the two boa constrictors
and his team of conspirators
who were selling guaranteed remedies

        for sexual impotency,
        for the sudden heart attack
        that killed your father,
        for varicose veins,
        for the upset stomach,
        for life itself,

and you believed every word he said
because you have rubbed elbows with poor people,
rich people and people in-between,

and in the midst of their bodies you caught
the faint whiff of all the meanings of love.
It was there, suddenly,
in the twilight
sometime after six in the midst
of the history of Mexico,

  there

    tangled
    among

the sweethearts stealing kisses on the park benches,
the babies huddled in their mothers' arms, that
peculiar old man walking his dog with the dangling broken leg,
the middle-aged couple strolling hand and hand
having just forgiven each other of all their many sins,

      there

in the shrill voices of venders hustling a living,
the money changing hands, there even
in the refrescos fríos, the helados y paletas,
melónes, papayas, mangos,
tacos ricos de todo tipo de guisados,
images of the Baby Jesus, images
of Jesus Christ truly suffering on the Cross,
Nuestra Señora de Guadalupe blessing us all,
color fotos of grandma and grandpa,
the belts, nail clippers, scotch tape, shampoo,
pens and pencils, Chiclets, newspapers and magazines,
a pair of shiny black shoes, size 12,
everything that you may possibly need
to live and die with
on a crowded Sunday afternoon
walking alone in the dream of
La Alameda Central

     But now you've made your promenade,
    and you're sitting at a table

just like any other customer
who enjoys the absolute white
of a table cloth at El Trevi.

Blas with the broad smile
is serving you the cappuccino in a glass
with a dash of cinnamon
floating on top the fluffy cream.
The people are still walking by the window.

    Life never quits,
        Blas whispers to you
            in Spanish,

and he says that it's okay if you die
in the morning maybe,
or next year, or whenever.
What difference would it truly make?
Isn't Diego dead, he asks?
And your friends Mike and Jimmy and David?
And Gail Brandon too?
                You stir the cappuccino
until the coffee, the steamed milk,
the cinnamon, the spoon,
the muscle and bone of your fingers and wrist—

they all become one thing
perfectly.
Maybe, you add a little sugar.
Still, the cappuccino is too hot.
You must wait.
In the waiting you get lost in your self
and you forget about Blas,
    but that's okay,
        that's part of the dream.

                Mexico City
                July 1994
                for Joe Hayes

*The title of this poem is the English translation of the title of
Diego Rivera's mural, *Sueño de una Tarde Dominical en la
Alameda Central*

Goodbye
Bobby Byrd

Ricardo took a look at his body
withered and yellow
cancerous rot
worthless loins
stench of hospital
reduced he was to perfection
his very self
Teresa entering the room

ding
      ding
            ding

angel cloth damp and cool
ti:le desert light like shine
on the side of a 1969 Impala
a .357 Magnum oiled
a silver dollar
watermelons
manstuff
Mexicans crossing the river
the eyeball of God
who it turned out
for the pure exercise
was a one-eyed woman
lived in one of those
roach infested apartments
off Paisano
did some curandera work

            Ricardo Sanchez

who always wanted to believe
thought for a few seconds

said in English
Fuck this
and he meant every word of it
so slipped he away
yesterday
Sunday the Lord's Day
September 3 1995
carried with himself into the darkness
the sweet smell of Teresa
those beautiful eyes
a snapshot of his kids grandkids
toda la familia
some jingle jangle for the santos
anillos pesados for every finger of the holiness Our Lady—
tiny black spot of rage that clung to his soul
a 1000 or so words in spanish
ditto the english

the lingo inbetween
una mezclada de syntactical secrets
the como se llama of poverty
freshly devised manifestos re: the democracy of divinity
a couple of useless names of friends to throw at the wind
neon blue pen red satin handkerchief
manual typewriter white paper a notebook
some crayons for Manny
garlic onions beans
Right rear haunch of northern new mexico venison
fresh tomatos
tortillas de maíz de méxico
the best bottle of tequila he could find
un cóctel molotov para buena suerte
organic coffee picked by communists
absolutely no money
curious grin
a fist
no
two fists
made of soft chicano hands
various hunks of silver jewelry turquoise red beaded necklace
etcetera

naked as the day he was born

emerged like that funny looking Indian saint

with a pack on his back

the bato stopped by my house

played a little tune on a penny whistle

and said goodbye

Understanding Korean
Marie Lee

It was moving day, and the last thing to be moved was posing problems. Mother sat in the middle of the bare apartment, her lips compressed into a straight line, Muppet-like.

"*Mother, there'll be lots of trees and grass where we're going,*" I murmured in my most wheedling Korean. "*You can plant a garden and grow* kochu *and* hobak."

"*What good is a garden if I have no friends?*" she said. The obstinate look on her face was unmoved. She looked like Sitting Bull.

I was thinking about how the movers were being paid by the hour, and how each moment was costing us needlessly. The movers were waiting outside with the truck, and I imagine they'd looked upon this whole afternoon with benign interest, the way people do at a foreign movie playing on the public monitors at a video store.

"Mother, we've got to go," I finally said. I hate using that tone with her, but we were going to end up in Barrington Park, New Jersey, even if she sat here all day.

"Please, Mother."

No response.

I picked my mother up, putting my hands under her armpits. She turned limp as old *kimchi* and her frail body suddenly seemed to weigh a ton, not to mention she appeared to be oozing out from between my hands. She could have been a sixties civil rights demonstrator, for all her savvy ways.

I managed to hold on until her feet met the floor. She would either have to stand up or crumple to the floor—I was counting on the former. A bead of sweat trailed like a snail from my temple to my cheek. If she fell—ended up in the hospital with a broken hip or worse—she would have every reason in the world to blame me, and she would. Life would become more complicated. We'd have to redo the house to accommodate it to a wheelchair. The car, too.

My hands fell away like dead leaves. I held my breath.

She stood.

"Now, that wasn't so hard, was it?" I patted her awkwardly on the shoulder, as if she were a pet. She didn't reply.

"I guess we're all packed up." Ashley's voice floated in from beyond the door.

"We're coming, I said cheerfully. Ashley wouldn't be fooled.

The moving company we've hired is called Yarmulke Movers. I see the men, black hair curly as a lamb's back, looking with mild interest as my mother and I emerge. Their eyes light up when they see my wife.

Ashley is as stunning as she was in her twenties. She's tall, but not taller than me. Her brown hair has lost some of its bronze glints, but it's still long and thick, and her hazel eyes are just as striking as the first time I encountered them at the card catalog of our college's library.

"Hae Ja," she says to my mother. "Do you think you'll be most comfortable in the front, where you can stretch your legs?"

Her tone is as caring and sweet as any mother-in-law could hope for, but I know Mother will only focus on the fact that Ashley has disrespectfully called her, an older person, by her given name.

Mother gets into the car with reluctant dignity, the way I imagine Marie Antoinette did for her last ride. Everything in her face reads, "you have brought me to America only to torture me," even though she is the one who came without waiting to be invited. I start up the car, trying to remember that moving from a cramped city apartment to a house in the suburbs is supposed to be a happy occasion.

Deanna, my oldest, pinches my shoulder from the back seat.

"What took you and Grandma so long?"

"Grandma had to go to the bathroom," I say. I have used this excuse so often that Alice, the younger of my daughters, believes her grandmother is incontinent.

The Yarmulke truck pulls away from the curb with a chuff of diesel smoke and a grinding of gears. I fall in behind it. "Say goodbye," I say. "Goodbye, apartment, goodbye!"

Ashley, Deanna, and Alice lean out the window and scream it. Mother is silent.

As we crawl uptown to the George Washington Bridge, I keep staring at the Yarmulke logo on the back of the truck. The way they painted it, it looks like a beanie, like they should put a propeller on it. I lean back to tell this to Ashley.

"You can customize them," she says knowingly. Ashley is the product of a mixed marriage, Christian and Jew. She became an agnostic so she wouldn't have to choose between her parents. "I've seen Bart Simpson yarmulkes."

"If I become Jewish, I'll get those," I tell her.

It's hard to believe that all our possessions—intimate and mundane—are packed away behind that door with the bad yarmulke painted on it: photo albums, rollerblades, coffee grinder, beds, shoe trees, med school textbooks (mine), books of torts (Ashley's), the girls' toys including Super Barbie Beach House and skis in all shapes and sizes.

As the truck gathers speed on the bridge. I imagine what it'd be like if the bridge suddenly opened up in front of us and the truck pitched headlong into the Hudson. The drivers would be neatly plucked out of the water by the Coast Guard, but the truck itself would sink, bubbles rising as it disappeared underwater.

Imagine the lightness. No tax records, CD collection. Kids' school records, bills, shower caddy. All gone.

But what would happen is that we'd have to file insurance forms. Buy things all over again. Get duplicates of records. It would only be a pain. That's how life worked. There was no more room for grand, sweeping gestures, starting over in unconquered territory. That stuff probably had only existed in the bootleg Louis L'Amour novels I'd read as a boy in Korea.

I was forty-one, had lived over half my life in America, and as far as I could see, everything had a safety net, which is a net all the same.

*

The yard of our new house is an expanse of green, like a mini-golf course. When the men were laying the sod, I asked them to leave a ten-by-ten plot for Mother's garden. She hasn't been outside yet think she'll be excited when she sees the freshly turned earth waiting for her.

That's what she needs, to feel wanted and useful. In the city, what was there to do? She hated to go out since her English is so rudimentary, and it wasn't as if there were tons of other Korean *halmoni* just hanging around the neighborhood. So unless one of the girls was sick or it was a school holiday, she would content herself with scrupulously cleaning the house—every day, including doing the laundry.

Ashley and I used to joke about Mother "kidnapping" our clothes. Ever since she moved in, if Ashley or I ever left a piece of clothing out—even if only to wear it later—it would mysteriously disappear and later reappear washed, pressed, and folded. Some of my primary-color polo shirts were starting to fade from being washed so much.

"I never know where half my stuff is," I complained, as I rooted around to find a polo shirt to wear with my jeans. "Either I lost it, it's hidden, or it's in the laundry—or all three."

"I think it's cute, the way your mother takes care of you," Ashley remarked, although I knew that she hid her lacy, sexy panties and those that got stained with her period so she could do them herself in the bathroom sink.

"You should never have taught her how to use to washing machine," I said.

"I didn't," Ashley answered. I must have looked incredulous because she gave me a tiny, wan smile and added, "honest."

Our first official new house celebration was a trip to the Sea Queen. The restaurant is only a few minutes away by car in the next town, Lester.

The girls were entranced from the moment they walked in the door.

Hey Dee, look at this," Alice exclaimed, pointing to a fake fish nailed to the wall.

"Cool," said Deanna, lengthening the word to two syllables: *coo* and *well*.

The maitre d's station had a ship's steering wheel mounted on it, making it appear that the tuxedoed man showing us our seats was also guiding the restaurant through spirited seas. Also cool.

Like my kids, this is the first time I'd ever been to a restaurant like this. In Korea, when visiting Cheju Island, I'd eaten octopus so fresh its tentacles were still wiggling. I've also had Maine lobster in Maine, sushi on the East Side. But these landlocked seafood restaurants were new to me. Ashley said the Sea Queen reminded her of her childhood in Phoenix, when they used to go to Red Lobster all the time.

Mother was the only one not showing any visible excitement about dining *chez* Sea Queen. In fact, she'd raised a fuss about going at all until we threatened to leave her at home.

"I'm going to have lobster," said Deanna, looking at all the people wearing plastic bibs.

"Co-ol," said Alice. "Me too."

"You girls sure you're going to like it?" I said, eyeing the twenty-dollar-plus price tag.

"How are we supposed to know?" Deanna said, rolling her eyes toward the faux-fishing nets suspended from the ceiling. A mermaid mannequin, clad only in a teeny seashell bra, floated above Mother's head. "We've never had lobster before, Daddy."

"Lobster feed on bad stuff at bottom of the sea," Mother said ominously. "Garbage eater." Alice looked shocked, and Deanna made a face. Why was it, I wondered, that when I encouraged my mother to do simple things that involved speaking English, such as asking for a loaf of bread at Key Food, she acted like I was asking her to split an atom in the kitchen sink? When it came to expressing unpleasant thoughts, she made herself only too clear.

Of course, it was a strange situation in the house, where no one could really talk to Mother except me. Had I known she was going to come to America, perhaps I would have talked to the girls in Korean when they were two or three, that age where kids' brains are like sponges with language. But at that time, I also had so many other things on my mind: getting through my internship, taking my licensing exam, raising two young daughters on the mean streets of New York. Establishing a solid practice so that I could move us all out here.

I remember when Mother got off that plane at Kennedy. The girls ran right up to her, and Mother stroked each of their heads, then looked up at me.

"*Aigu, the children don't speak Korean?*" was the first thing my mother said to me.

"No, Mother."

Immediately, my mother gave the fish-eye to my very Caucasian wife, who looked back at me with puzzlement.

"She says she's tired from such a long and hot flight," I said.

Ashley had been all graciousness. She gently took Mother's heavy bags—loaded with all sorts of Korean food—and led her to the car. Alice and Deanna, seven and eight at the time, followed obediently, staring with fascination at this little old lady shuffling through the terminal like an Asian Yoda.

When I had announced my intention to marry Ashley and stay in America, my mother promptly declared that the news would kill my father. My only recourse would be to come home right away—then and only then would I have a chance to earn forgiveness. I called them again to say I would stay with Ashley.

Father died of a stroke less than a year later. I suppose my mother blamed it on me, although I don't know for sure because we never talked about it. I knew they were serious in their opposition to the marriage, and even expected they might boycott the ceremony. But I never expected them to disown me.

The next time I called, Mother said she had no son. Then she hung up and did not pick up the phone when I rang again. I never spoke to my father again, only heard the news of his death from a distant aunt.

Ashley knew everything that had gone on. I told her. I was careful not to make it into a big deal, like I had given up everything for love, but I admit there were times when the sacrifice, this big pulsating creature, would sit itself down like an elephant in the middle of the house, inescapable. Like the time when Alice came home from school and said, "Janey has two grandma and grandpas. So does Amy. How come we only have Grandma and Grandpa Schlos?"

But who could have predicted the inexplicable turn of events, when Mother called to say she was coming to America. Even though I regularly sent her money (unacknowledged, but unreturned), she had decided that it was too difficult to live in Korea with so few relatives around.

She said she was going to come live with us.

Our lives changed irrevocably that day we drove out to pick her up. But I try not to think too deeply about it, about whether the change was good or bad. I think what I'm most afraid of is that I'll find I have no more love for my mother, that my heart is only a dried husk, that under the harsh light of introspection, we would see that the mother-son bond consisted of duty only, nothing more.

"You should try the bouillabaisse," I said, leaning in toward Mother, who was perusing the heavy decoupaged leaves of the menu before her. I'd suggested that because bouillabaisse was very much like a Korean soup, the name of which I suddenly couldn't recall.

I had blackened tuna, dry and burnt as a piece of toast. I had managed to convince the girls to order only one lobster. They oohed and aahed when it came, prostrate and newly reddened as a beached tourist. They squealed with joy while cracking off the claws and dipping the pale meat into butter, although I could tell from their faces they weren't entirely pleased with the taste.

The waiter came and showed them how to open the shell to get the meat of the abdomen. As he tore into the carapace, a torrent of gluey, green liquid shot out.

Deanna screamed.

The waiter grinned. "This is special stuff," he said.

"Gourmets like to see lots of green. It's your lucky day."

Neither girl touched the lobster after that. Ashley and I dutifully tried to eat as much as we could of the remains, which tasted fine, despite the green stuff. A little less than half the lobster was left on the plate. Mother watched knowingly.

"Mother, it's almost June—why don't you plant something in your garden?" I asked her one day as she prepared me breakfast: eggs and toast. She always served me, then left whatever remained for Ashley and the kids. Ashley never complained about getting leftovers.

"The seeds and tools are in the garage," I added. Weekly, during our time in the city, Mother had always spoken of how, if she could only have a garden, she would plant carrots, *hobak* squash, beans, and *kochu* peppers. So I'd gone out to the local garden store and bought all the seeds and materials. I'd even found seeds for a pepper plant that looked, from its photo on the Burpee seed packet, remarkably like the *kochu* peppers we had grown on our balcony back in Korea. But the ground still waited, drying on the edges.

She shrugged. "*Maybe.*"

I took this to be a good sign.

Weekends totally changed when Mother came into our lives. Before, Ashley and I, nonchurchgoers both, looked forward to Sundays as the day we had sex. When the girls were small, it was a piece of cake. But even as they grew, we just looked upon it as a challenge.

Sometimes, we awoke extra early, then we would lie satiated in damp nightclothes and acted, when the girls stirred, as if we were just waking up. Sometimes we did it quickly, fiercely, putting our hands over each other's mouths, and we were up at our normal time, full of energy.

We once thought about putting a lock on the door, but we decided against it; we didn't like the symbolism of shutting the girls out, and they never barged in anyways; both girls tended to sleep like logs on the weekends.

But once Mother moved in, I thought about the locks again. Her first Sunday with us, she curtly asked us why we were so late in getting up, and I looked up to see her eyes boring into ours. Ashley blushed her splotchy blush, and I knew she knew, too. She called it "understanding Korean."

Or there was the time we were making love and Ashley's period had started unexpectedly and we bloodied the sheets before we knew it. After surveying the mess, instead of laughing and tossing it in the washer with mischievous grins, we carefully, almost shamefully, hid the sheets by stuffing them into the bottom of a box, on top of which we piled shoes. Later, we realized there would be no way to wash them without Mother seeing, so we threw the sheets out, still in the box.

I remember thinking, why are we doing this, hiding from my mother the fact we have sex?—and we already have two children!

Needless to say, Sundays hadn't been the same since she arrived. Even being in a bigger house didn't help. Each squeak, every rustle seemed to reverberate straight down to Mother's room, and she would take it upon herself to get up, pad toward our room, then veer off to the bathroom. Sometimes, I would keep staring at the door with horrid fascination, waiting for the knob to turn right when I entered Ashley. It was right out of a Hitchcock movie.

Now, I'm trying to get Mother to join a Korean Church out here. An inelegant, imperfect solution, but I think it could work. When I mentioned the idea to her, she did not say no. In fact, she said I should have been more considerate and tried to find her one earlier.

On this Sunday, we are all sitting in the kitchen—windows flung open wide into the suburban breezes—staring at the *New York Times*. Mother is still in bed.

"Goddamnit!"

The word floats, through the crisp white eyelet curtains.

"You crazy or something, lady?"

I frown. The voice seems to be coming from the direction of our neighbor on the left. Our neighbors to the right have already greeted us, but we've not yet, after all these months, met the person on the left, even though we've stopped by several times.

"Swearing up a storm on a Sunday," I remark, but everyone is buried in different sections of the paper.

Suddenly, there is pounding on the front door. Ashley rises with a sigh to get it.

"Do you guys mind?" An irritated voice enters the house in waves, like smoke. "Tell that old lady to quit it. You're making my blood pressure shoot through the roof."

The rest of us hear Ashley murmur something and shut the door.

"It's Mother," she says. "In the backyard."

In the backyard? Impossible? How could Mother creep past us without someone noticing?

But there she is, standing up on a lawn chair near the fence. She is partially obscured by the huge rhododendron bush Ashley has just planted.

She is holding up seedy dandelions and blowing their fuzzy heads apart, aiming her breeze right into the neighbor's yard. She doesn't look like she's making a wish. Instead, she looks robotic, determined. Inhale, blow. Inhale, blow. A slight flush has come to her cheeks with the effort.

"*Mother*," I say in Korean.

"*It's a free country*," she says, blowing apart another head. The seeds float off like tiny, brave paratroopers into the occupied territory of our new neighbor's yard.

His name is Mr. Rudolph, and he is there with us, observing the whole thing. I am suddenly seized with the fear he is going to say something racist to us—race seems to always poke its ugly head into disputes like this. It's an easy way to release anger.

...I'm toodling along the turnpike and some guy thinks I cut in front of him. So of course he yells "chink!" Or I'm shopping at the supermarket, and I accidentally give the old grandma in front of me a bump with the cart. She immediately tells me to go back where I came from, her voice sounding like a drill sergeant's.

But Mr. Rudolph says nothing. In fact, I think he sees how helpless and exasperated I am, and he is a model of restraint. I vow to buy a gallon of Weed-B-Gone and clean up his lawn.

"We can't go on like this," I tell Ashley, as we're lying in bed that night.

"Like what?" she asks me, gently.

"I'm supposed to be the filial son and take care of my mother forever...aaahhh....." I let my voice trail off, as if I'm falling off a cliff.

"And..?" she prompts. She knows there's more.

"I don't know if I love her."

This comes out unexpectedly, the way a fish can fall from the middle of a clear sky after a tornado. I wait for Ashley to scream "monster!" and turn me out of bed. She merely rolls over, puts a hand on my chest.

"Mmm, smooth," she says. Has she heard me? Her hand moves lower.

"So what should we do?" I say weakly, as I realize the ultimate goal of her hand's journey.

"I think," she says, stopping to plant a kiss, "you shouldn't stress about things you can't do anything about."

Her saying this only makes me more tense, like there must be something I should feel guilty about: I must figure out what it is and begin feeling guilty immediately.

"I know something that relieves stress." The pressure of her fingers increases. The more primitive parts of my brain crowd out the others. Yaargh, I am thinking. Yarrgh.

I look to the bedroom door, wishing again, that we had a lock on it. Tomorrow. Maybe tomorrow.

I am overjoyed to discover that there is a Korean church in nearby Stillwell—and Mother wants to go. However, she insists that I go with her, at least for the first time. I agree; I'd agree to just about anything at this point.

That morning, a sweet, fresh breeze is blowing in, the scent of flowers from the garden riding on top. Ashley's arms are warm, and I imagine all sorts things—for a minute—then I push myself out of bed and start hunting for a tie.

Stillwell looks like a clone of Barrington Park—grass, neatly trimmed shrubs, a street of one or two cute shops for totally useless pursuits like needlepoint or sponge painting.

But Stillwell has Korean Church, and Barrington Park doesn't.

At the parking lot of the church, I help my mother out even though she does not need it. She lets me. Other people are emerging from their vehicles and heading to the church. This is the first time, I realize, that I've been around so many Koreans since Korea.

In fact, at our wedding, there had been only one Korean guest, my college friend Andy Kim. The whole affair had been rushed and casual and spontaneous. Ashley made the invitations on her Mac at work and sent them out on company letterhead envelopes. A schoolteacher friend gave us the keys to his school's gymnasium. All the guests wore sneakers. We danced and drank and then crammed into our apartment for potluck supplemented by Chinese takeout and supermarket beer. In some ways, it was not like a real wedding. Ashley's parents went home before the celebration moved into its second phase. I didn't miss my parents. Really.

Before we'd left this morning, Mother complained it would be hard to join a new church, something about the complicated social networks that somehow survive the journey all the way from Korea. Now that she was actually at the church, she looked around warily, perhaps the way a new tiger does when it's introduced to its mates at the zoo. People—men in their shiny dark suits, women in their brightly colored dresses, children looking far too scrubbed to be real children—looked at us.

We sat down in the pews. The people next to us nodded slightly. A good sign.

Then there was a load groaning noise that almost made me shoot out of my seat. It sounded again.

B-A-A-R-R-R-N-G.

The *jing*. That mournful gong-type bell. I remember now, those sleepy mornings sitting on hard pews and being jolted by that sound, as if it were my spine, not the thick metal, being struck.

The service was conducted in Korean, and I realized how rusty my language had become. I know I did almost everything in English—think, dream, talk—but I always thought that Korean would always remain the prime mover, since that's what took up residence in my brain first.

I still spoke it with Mother, but only about the most basic things, the children or what we're having for dinner. I wondered if Mother noticed my slippage. I'd been sent here to learn English, but was it also possible to lose some of that which I came with?

When the minister asked new members to introduce themselves, I thought I'd have to prod Mother, but she stood up on her own.

"I am Kim Nam Soon," she said in a clear voice. *"I am from Seoul, although I crossed over from North Korea to the South in 1945. And now I am here, in America with my son."*

The minister smiled kindly at her. The people next to us nodded their heads with approval. I suddenly had questions to ask her, but of course it was church, and you had to be quiet.

At the social hour, I stood by while people jammed around Mother and spoke in a Korean that sprinted so quickly by me that I often could not hold onto it.

"This is my son," she said proudly to each new person. I noticed that some of them looked at my wedding band with curiosity. I would smile, nod slightly, and bow.

When we came home, I was surprised to see Mr. Rudolph in our kitchen.

"Mr. Rudolph was mowing his lawn," Ashley explained. "So I invited him in for iced tea."

Mr. Rudolph and Mother exchanged sour looks. I thought of the thick-rooted dandelions that were probably germinating under his sod right now; little time bombs that would soon choke his yard with back-breaking tenacity.

Guiltily, I escaped upstairs on the pretext of changing my clothes.

When I returned, I found Mother and Mr. Rudolph talking animatedly while Ashley tidied up in the background.

"So you can see how old I am," Mr. Rudolph said, intently gazing at the fingerprints he made in the condensation of his glass. "I remember it being real real cold in Korea. They didn't call us the Chosun Frozen for nothing."

"Old nothing," Mother sputtered. "I walk over the border in 1945—right into South Korea."

I sat down heavily. I'd always thought our family was from Seoul; I never knew we had any ties to the North. And now Mother had mentioned it twice today, with no prompting, and to complete strangers.

"I was carrying my son here," Mother said, vaguely gesturing my way. "He big then too, huh! He cry so much that the ones I with say we leave him behind, cannot take no chances. It was very dangerous there, many soldier."

Deanna and Alice suddenly burst inside. They shuffled to the table to filch cookies, then lingered.

"So what happened?" Mr. Rudolph looked thoroughly entranced.

"I go out on my own," she said. "Many danger, not just soldier but also bandit—lots of refugees carry family jewel and gold—and there tiger, too. I stick my finger in baby's mouth so he can suck as we make way."

"Wasn't he heavy?" Ashley interjected. Mother looked at her, as if she'd just seen her for the first time.

"Oh yes," Mother flapped her arms up and down at the memory. "Very heavy, like sack of rice," she said. "But when you run for life, he felt like feather. He no cry, everything turn out okay."

It was just now that I was realizing that Mother had made this conversation totally in English. I wondered if she could see the pride coming out of my ears. Alice edged closer to Mother to nab another cookie. Their arms brushed. Mother's hand fluttered up briefly—a bird alighting on a branch—and stroked Alice's straight hair.

"Your father," Mother said, looking at me. "Already in South, he wait. But then I no show up two, three days after others. He think for sure we two dead."

I never noticed before how strong and straight my mother's posture is, even if she is only about five feet tall. Alice, in all her preadolescent coltish glory, looks positively slouchy next to her. Mr. Rudolph stays on, until it's almost too late to finish mowing his lawn.

"*Mother, how come you never told me any of this before?*" I asked her, later, under the private cover of Korean.

She just shrugged. Deanna was studying at the kitchen table, Alice was playing Nintendo next to her. Ashley was peering into her laptop computer. The scene looked like some yuppie commercial for life insurance or Volvos. But it made me happy.

"*Maybe I didn't want to make you feel bad,*" Mother said, finally.

"*Bad like what?*"

"*Like when you didn't come back to Korea.*"

Had I known my mother had done this for me, I wonder if I would have still stayed here against her wishes. Possibly not. Quite possibly not.

So why did she keep this weapon hidden in her arsenal when she had used so many others? "Your father will die if you don't come home. We can't believe we raised you, the most unfilial and ungrateful son. You are a shame to our family."

It made me think of my first patient who had died. He had sliced his leg with a chainsaw, and it seemed the amputation was going to be the biggest tragedy of his life. But then there was the freak unexplained thrombosis—a clot—that made its way to his heart and killed him. While he was mourning the loss of his leg, too many other things went unappreciated.

"*Thank you, Mother,*" I said, in my most respectful Korean, and I got on the floor and did a deep bow, the kind I hadn't done since I was a child, on New Year's. Deanna gave Alice a rolled eyed "what's Daddy doing?" look, as they watched me practically burying my face in the carpet, but neither said anything.

I wonder what my kids are going to think of me when they get older. I have always thought of my parents more as wardens of my prison than any object deserving of love. It was always study harder, you are too stupid, we are sending you across the ocean to learn English and go to college because you are too stupid to get into college here. But now we want you to come back. You won't come back? We disown you.

Ashley and her mother are always hugging each other, and saying "I love you" and holding hands. This is not my mother's way. I try to imagine her hands in 1945, strong, loving, as she refused to let go of me, even when I cried. Even when her life was in danger, when everyone else had left her.

"When I die, you will do your duty at my grave, yes?" Mother says to me.

I lean forward and take her hand. It feels like watered silk—so much softer than it looks. At first she looks startled, but then relaxes into my grip. How exasperating this woman, I think, talking about *josang*, ancestor worship, after spending the whole morning in church.

"I'll do even better than that, Mother," I say. *"I'll worship you while you're still alive."*

I happen to glance over at Ashley, and our eyes meet. She smiles as if she's understood what I've said, and approves.

Light Witness
Darrell Bourque

(after scenes from *For a Lost Soldier*)

I was crying and it was raining. I was outside with my sister who was hanging clothes in the rain. I was screaming at her that she had ruined the film, that I would never have the photograph, that he had become my friend. How would I remember him when he went back to where he had come from? How would I know what he looked like? How would I be able to remember that when he saw us lined up to have the picture made, he broke away from his friends and into our line to stand next to me. How would I remember if I couldn't see him that he had put his arm around me, his right hand on my upper right arm as we stood and smiled for the other soldier to take the picture. This is the way the soldiers touched each other in their pictures. He had made me one of them when he put his arm around me like that. Now, I was saying to her, I can still feel his hand on my arm. Now, I can still hear his friends calling his name with the three heavy sounds, each sound as heavy as stone pushed through the frozen ground in the spring. I can still hear him saying to me as we sat at the table in the farmhouse he and the other soldiers were staying in: *You could be an artist with those hands.* I can still hear his low, even voice saying that to me right now, but a week from now, a month, a year, when I am his age, how will I remember that he said all that, and that he said *the hands make what the mind sees* if I cannot see him any more? How will I remember riding the bike over the low wetlands to see him if I can't see where I'm going any more, if I can't smell the air with him in it, if I can't see the lightness he went away from us in? How will I know how to play with the scarecrow he put in the photograph if the scarecrow is in my head and it is scaring everything away and I cannot get in my head to take it out so that it doesn't scare him away, so that we don't scare him away because none of us can see him anymore?

Physics Report
Darrell Bourque

It is the end of the lovebug season
here in south Louisiana.
We are taking teflon-wrapped sponges
to our windshields and to the bumpers
of our cars.
        In northern New Zealand a mountaintop blows.
The ash takes with it a lake.
The water no longer certifiable
or measurable as what it was.
a deep blue bowl in thin air.
        I know more than nothing about
Lorenz's initial condition effect
on weather systems theory.
I know more than nothing about
energy field physics,
but I like the idea of poets calibrating
the energy in the lines of what they make
and scientists getting out their calipers
to measure the fat content in images.
    In Miss Dixie Wynn's sixth hour class just last week
the testosterone levels, she says were unchartable.
It was as if some gorgeous cajun blonde Medusa had turned
this boy-filled class to charged stone.
Empirically speaking, three weeks after
the beginning of the fall term
Elizabeth Broussard's schedule changed.
Ben Bernard wrote an essay
on a person who most influenced him
and he wrote about his uncle
he works with.
He said his uncle was teaching him a trade.
That it was more than learning how to be a cabinet maker.
It was about how to smooth surfaces
and how to make angles fit.
It was about how to make things
strong so that no one ever noticed

how strong a thing was.
It was about dovetails and miter boxes.
And then he said it was, too,
about how his uncle was teaching him
how to be a good father and a good husband,
and he didn't know where that last thing came from
and he wondered what connections, if any,
all that had to do with what Miss Dixie had been saying
one day about something that sounded like *plague*
that you couldn't do when you write,
and then something about your writing
having to be about you and having to be true
and it seemed to him that this line in his essay
about a father and husband was both of those things
and besides that he didn't know why
he kept seeing Elizabeth about to turn
around in his writing-log entries.
Her long blond hair moving.
Her turning her face to him.
Her eyes the color of deep mountain lake water.
Him, some father, some husband
swimming in them
         Just before he closes his eyes for the last time
Hokusai releases thirty-six variations of each
of his *Thirty-Six Views of Mount Fuji.*
         This morning at the edge of a pine grove
near the emperor's retreat the mist barely touches
the tops of the boulders in the garden.
The caretaker is raking the gravel.
The imperial embroiderers are taking notes
on the pinks in the peonies blooming.
    A hummingbird near the rim of the Atchafalaya Basin
is making its way to the red mallows,
the subscription in its wings,
                Kyoto, Kyoto, Kyoto
its heart's hurried aria,
              *yokuboo, yokuboo, yokuboo.**

*desire

American Meltdown
Dixie Salazar

Angel's in love
with this white girl
who props her Nikes
on the Rush bumper sticker
of her father's Volvo.
She taunts him
with the pale swish
of her ponytail
and washed out eyes.
Angel reaches for her
through twilight fire
and the diamonds
of her father's chain link.

At night, an albino moon
drives him mad
with blonde circulations.
Giving in to an old
gravitational pull,
he knots his body
into white bedsheets.
It's nothing new,
the easy attraction
of bipolar winds,
the absence of light
seeking light, the desire
to conquer the conqueror.
He wakes in the cold
bath of his own heat.

He ducks, then accepts
the blows she rains
on his head, throws
his history book to the wind,
lets the simple juice
of spring fill him

like every stem and vein
in gold confusion.
Watering the hydrangea
after dinner, I watch
their dance of fire,
the sky filled with the sparks
of their contact.

I think of my father
who buys American cars,
married Anglo like his brothers,
and now his great-grandchildren
are only one-eighth of him,
no one speaks Spanish,
and the melt-down is complete.

In a dizzy whoop
of love and pain, Angel
calls to her. Their arms
tangle dark and light.
Half of me
wants him to stop,
to untangle, pull back
into the safety of shadows,
and half of me wants him
to melt with her
in the crucible of lost light,
to reach the fusing point
of a new element,
to loose himself
in the cold alchemy of the heart.

This Black Stone
Homero Aridjis

This black stone
Is a piece of night
That time has made palpable
So that a man
Can take up darkness in his hand

Translated by Gregory McNamee.

When Contepec is Nothing More in the Night
Homero Aridjis

When Contepec is nothing more in the night
than a stone
and the villages surrounding it
no more than names
the Altamirano plateau will be
the shadow of a wounded bird
in the golden dawn
crossing for a moment
the ever-present emptiness

Translated by Gregory McNamee.

Greenland
Sylvia Mullen Tohill

The winter I am nine, my mother loses all sense of reality. When my grandfather holds up the snapshot of the McLoughlins, the snow is climbing clear to the eaves behind them and their bodies are swallowed up by the coats they're wearing. But my mother isn't looking at that. All she sees is their faces, beaming as if small suns shone inside them, warming the McLoughlins so they don't even need those heavy parkas.

Come and visit, they say in the letter, and when I look at my mother, I think she's already gone there. Beside the dining room table with a sack of groceries in her arms, she is looking far off through the bay windows, her eyes set on a place that hadn't existed until the McLoughlins sent us this photo. She has forgotten how far it is from Mayesville, Colorado, to Juneau, Alaska.

My grandfather has gone off with her. Around and around the dining room table he marches with my two brothers behind him, singing Alaska's state song and waving the miniature flag the McLoughlins have sent us.

My mother comes back to her senses. Already it's past 5:30 and she has groceries to put away before she cooks dinner, ironing to do before bedtime.

But upstairs where we've lived since my father died, she stands at the kitchen stove and talks to herself out loud. "Juneau," she whispers as if it were the name of someone she'd loved and hadn't seen in a long time.

The next afternoon, when she has put up the last of the mail, she goes out the side door of the Mayesville Post Office and into the library behind it, searching for information about the place the McLoughlins have moved to. While her clerk is selling stamps and handing out packages on the other side of the partition, my mother and the librarian, a woman with one green eye and one brown one, are standing side by side, their two fingers moving like antenna along the yellowed spines of old *National Geographic* magazines, feeling their way toward the word Alaska.

In the evening, she piles a stack of magazines and books on the end table beside the sofa in the room that is our kitchen and living room. All winter their musty smell permeates the air, embedding itself into my perceptions of Alaska so when I'm grown and travel there alone, I will be startled when I step off the plane and breathe in the cool, fresh smell of sea and pine-clad mountains.

On the kitchen table, my two brothers unfold the Conoco map and draw a line in red crayon from southwest Colorado to Juneau, Alaska. We look again and again at the pictures in *National Geographic*. In her brown spiral notebook, my mother writes down the distance from Mayesville to Juneau and from there to Dawson Creek and Whitehorse and Fairbanks. She figures the price of a tent and the cost of food to get to the McLoughlins, then doubles the cost "in case," she says, "we decide to go even further."

When I ask her if we're really going, she looks surprised, as if I hadn't been listening.

"When?" I insist, but she frowns as if this were just another aspect of the trip she hasn't planned yet.

From the bedroom my mother and I share, I can hear my brothers in their room talking of dog sleds and polar bears and fishing for salmon. In the dark, while my mother speaks of totem poles and glaciers as large as mountains, I come to believe in the sleek bodies of whales that can erupt high into the air and glide back into the ocean.

What my grandparents talk about is the long summer days without darkness. They look again and again at the pictures of cabbages so large one of them fills a basket, but when we ask if they want to go with us, my grandfather says someone has to stay home and tend the garden and feed the chickens.

At school, I do my geography report on Alaska. I take in all the magazines and books we've gathered. I read excerpts from the McLoughlins' letters and show my classmates all the pictures they've sent. By the end of the report, I am so excited I tell the whole class something I haven't told anyone, except my friend Carolyn.

"We're going there," I whisper and, walking back to my desk, I think all their faces are set on mine, transfixed as if they, too, were going to Alaska.

In the backyard, we build an igloo with help from the other neighborhood children. When we have stacked great blocks of snow into a round room with a tunnel, my grandfather pours a bucket of water over the whole structure. In the late afternoon sunlight, it is a white domed ice palace that gleams so fiercely we have to squint when we look at it.

"*Wunderbar*," my grandfather says, and all of us laugh as if something had happened even more magical than we'd expected. In line, waiting to go inside, the boys bump each other's shoulders and shout my grandfather's word over and over while we girls smile at each other as if we don't know what to do with ourselves now that the igloo is finished. Beside the fence in his high buckled black overshoes, my grandfather watches us crawl into the igloo's tunnel, then applauds each time we come out, as if going inside the igloo took us so far away he never expected to see us again.

The igloo is so small only two of us can go in at a time. We sit with our knees tucked under our chins and our heads bent far forward. We plan bigger igloos with multiple rooms and a fire in the center where we can warm our hands, igloos so large we can live in them if we want to.

At night, I dream of reindeer running along the road beside us. Every face I see is the face of an Eskimo who looks out from the hood of a fur-lined coat, smiling. Inside my head I have words I've never had before this: Mukluks. Kayaks. Alexander Archipelago.

And then in the kitchen, on an evening at the end of January, it all stops. While I'm drying the dishes, I lift my head and see a look on my mother's face that hasn't been there since the first letter came from the McLoughlins, a look she wears when she's balancing the checkbook or trying to decide whether we're ill enough to take to the doctor, a look I had not seen for so long, I thought it no longer existed.

"Mother," I say, but she has her foot on the brake as surely as if she'd been driving us down the highway and realized how dark it was and how far we still were from Mayesville. She's turning the car around, hurrying us home before we've even left it.

At the table, my brothers are arguing about who shot the most baskets at recess, but she isn't listening to anything anyone is saying. She's looking through the glass doors to the porch, her eyes set on snow and gray sooted roofs, and the long months of winter still waiting beyond them.

"We aren't going," I say.

"It's a long ways," my mother says. Her hands grapple for something in the bottom of the dish-pan that slips away each time her fingers come near.

"And we're not going, are we?" I say, and now even my brothers are silent.

"Some day," she says, but she doesn't look at me.

"When?" I insist, determined not to give in until she sets a time.

"We need a more dependable car," she says. In the dishwater, her hands have stopped searching. Her head is up, but her eyes are set on the blank wall beside the picture of the Mendenhall Glacier as if directions were written there that all along she should have been reading.

"And more in savings," she says quietly and I can see it as clearly as if savings were a bully standing on the corner with his hand out, demanding more than we can ever give him.

"The Alcan Highway isn't even paved yet to Juneau," she says. Although it will be seven years before I'll be old enough to drive and eight and nine years before my brothers will be, she says if we wait, the three of us can help with the driving.

At the table, my brothers have their hands around imaginary steering wheels, squealing around curves and roaring down mountains. Already I have thrown the dishtowel on the table. I would go out the door but my brothers' chairs block it. While I am running into the hall, the place named Juneau has already lifted like a flock of white feathered birds and is trailing Fairbanks and Dawson and the whole western coastline of the United States and Canada behind it, flying so far away by the time I reach the bedroom, nothing is left of it but a thin line like smoke against the horizon.

In the kitchen, my brothers' voices are back on the basketball game as if nothing had happened, my mother as silent as if she'd disappeared all together.

On my bed with only a little space between it and my mother's, I tell myself I'm too old to be sleeping in the same room with my mother. I hate living all crowded together in the upstairs of a house. I long for a door I can open and slam closed behind me.

From where I sit, I can see that the stack of books and magazines about Alaska is no longer on the end table beside the sofa. All evening I lie on my bed and plan what I'll say when my mother comes into the bedroom, my words like our outside steps with a thin coat of ice all over them.

But my mother comes into the bedroom and sighs when she lies down as if her bed were so deep she won't be able to climb out again in the morning, and I keep all the hateful words I intended to say stored up inside me.

The rest of the winter, we speak no more about it. When the snow at the edges of buildings has disappeared, one smoke-grayed side of the igloo standing like a wall of an Indian ruin, I think everyone else has forgotten or never cared about going to Alaska. Letters from the McLoughlins are further and further apart. If my mother ever thinks of Juneau, her face doesn't show it.

My grandfather says no more of cabbages. Nightly he studies seed catalogs and reads about a new kind of tomato he wants to plant instead of the Big Boys he's always planted. While I dress for school in the mornings, I can hear him downstairs singing a song about blue mountain flowers in place of the song about Alaska.

My mother says when school is out we'll visit my cousins just like always. All day we'll ride inside our old gray Plymouth over Wolf Creek Pass and through the long hot San Luis Valley headed for Greenland, Colorado, a land that's green only because my uncle and my aunt irrigate the fields and carry water to the garden.

Whenever anyone in my family mentions Greenland, I am silent, ashamed to be part of a family so willing to replace a trip to Alaska with a visit to eastern Colorado.

On the last day of school, when I pass my teacher's desk on the way out to recess and she asks where we'll be going for vacation, I whisper the word "Greenland" as if it were the mournful word "nowhere" and I the only one who has to say it.

But Mrs. Folkert is delighted. "That's wonderful," she says. And, though I am surprised, her excitement is contagious. While I'm running across the playground, my cousins' back door opens and my cousin Julie is standing there inside it. In my uncle's pockets are pennies for us to lay on the railroad tracks that run on two sides of the farm. Streamliners are flying past us, transforming the coins into copper-colored curls that gleam all over the hillside.

I'm already sliding head first down the highest slide on the playground, my body in one place and my mind already in another, when I see Susan Pendleton standing at the bottom of the slide in her yellow Easter dress.

"Move," I call, but she stays where she is, her arms crossed over the front of her body, her face turned up toward me, her lips pinching together tighter and tighter. At the last moment she steps back, but when I swing my legs around and stand up, she is sneering as if she'd caught me doing something I shouldn't have been doing. A cluster of girls is standing behind her.

"Liar," Susan whispers, and the girls stumble back a little as if afraid they were who she was attacking.

Behind her, Carolyn is looking past me, her eyes searching the top of the schoolhouse stairs for a teacher who might come and stop what's about to happen. I know already that this is more serious than who Carolyn will play with after school.

I've never been called a liar before, but Susan's face and the face of nearly every girl behind her have already determined I'm guilty.

"Let's ask Laura where she's going now," she says to the girls, and their eyes turn small and glassy like chickens who've just discovered a wound on one of the other chickens.

I think this must be about the trip to Alaska and a way for Susan to get even with me for being best friends with Carolyn who is her cousin, things I can't defend myself against even if Susan would listen.

But Susan isn't finished. She presses her face so close to mine I can smell the sweet, fruity gum she's chewing. "Gruen," she says in a voice so high and warbly I can't understand what she's trying to say, and then before I can decipher that strange sound, she makes another sound. "Lunt," I think she says, and immediately laughter is dropping like a handful of pebbles around us.

On the playground the other children are racing about, hurrying up the steps to the slide and whooping down it, but where I stand, there is quiet, a quiet so permeated by dust and heat, I think I'll choke if I breathe it.

Susan's eyes are like the obsidian my brother Paul keeps on his dresser. I search every face behind her, looking for a face that will deny my shame or explain it, but I see only one thing clearly: this is about something so hideous no one can look at me.

At the edge of the group, even Carolyn has her head down. Beside the slide, she is kneeling, pulling soft green stickers out of her stockings. When she stands up, she keeps her eyes on the ground as if more stickers might leap up from that packed earth and attach themselves to her stockings, though no stickers have ever grown there before this.

And then, inside my head the two sounds come together. Susan has overheard what I said to our teacher. I see now why the teacher has responded with such pleasure and why Susan would exaggerate the word when she says it.

In their minds, Greenland is a snow-covered island where penguins and seals live, a place like Alaska, a place so unlike the place I'm actually going to, no one would confuse them.

I want it to be as simple as that. But when I look at Susan, her arms crossed, the yellow ribbon that matches her dress holding one perfect curl at the side of her head, I'm certain it isn't. No matter what I say now, the group will toss their heads and go off with their arms around each others' shoulders without me.

"I am going to Greenland," I tell them. I put both hands on my hips. I say the word "Greenland" without distorting it the way Susan had, but I don't add the word Colorado.

Behind Susan, Carolyn's face is so pale all I can see are her freckles and her wide eyes looking into mine as if she were the one lying and only my silence can save her.

High up on the porch of the yellow school building behind us, the recess bell is clanging, but I stay where I am, head up, my eyes daring every face that passes to call me a liar.

All the way across the playground and up the stairs, I tell myself regardless of what my mother does or of what Susan and the rest of them think, someday I *will* go to Alaska and to Greenland, the real Greenland.

When the school day is over, Carolyn lays a note on my desk that says I'm still her best friend, but she follows Susan out the door without looking at me. I fold the note over and over until it fits inside the place where the eraser has fallen out of my pencil, and then I throw it and the old pencil into the trash along with everything else I tell myself I don't need any longer.

But in my grandmother's kitchen, while I eat her sugar cookies and drink lemonade and answer her questions about the last day of school, I'm still three blocks away, walking down the street behind Carolyn and Susan, shrinking at the sound of their high, startled laughter.

While my grandfather comes into the kitchen and unpacks the groceries, setting each item out on the table and announcing its price to my grandmother, I'm in the office behind the showroom where Susan's father sells cars, imagining my best friend and Susan eating Hershey bars and whirling each other around in his chair.

At the table, my grandfather takes his largest butcher knife and slices a thin slab of longhorn cheese for each of us. He wraps the orange circle of cheese, a moon with waxy edges, back in the slick white paper and takes it into the pantry where he will hide it far back in the refrigerator as if it were a Christmas package.

While I eat my cheese, I'm certain Susan's father has already reached far down into his pocket and handed out nickels so Susan and Carolyn can run across the street to the Mayesville Grocery and buy soda pop. My mouth is full of my grandfather's cheese and my grandmother's lemonade, but I'm thinking about the taste of Hershey bars mixed with Coca Cola.

"No bananas?" my grandmother asks, and from the pantry my grandfather says, "Green." "Too green," he repeats as if he thinks she may not have heard him, but I'm hearing something else. At the bottom of the slide, Susan is saying the word exactly like my grandfather has just said it, her voice high and disgusted.

"It's all right," my grandmother says as if there were nothing strange about my grandfather's pronunciation. Already she's preparing to make apple instead of banana cream pie for dinner.

In the pantry, my grandfather is singing the old hymn "Bringing in the Sheaves," singing so loudly I think everyone in the neighborhood will hear him rolling the words together as if they were one long, hyphenated word, their edges all blurred together.

And then I see the possibility of something else as clearly as if I had ridden to town with my grandfather in his old brown Dodge.

Three blocks away on Main Street, when he got out of his car and crossed the street in his Sunday hat and the old overalls he wears in the garden, Susan and Carolyn were probably still in the Mayesville Grocery.

"Well, well, well," my grandfather is saying at the table beside me, but what I hear fills me with such dread I want him to stop talking altogether: at the beginning of a word that should start with "w," he has put a "v" sound. He pulls his pocket watch out of his overalls and looks at its face.

"Tomorrow, at this time, you should be in Greenland," he says, and the word Greenland rumbles as if he were exaggerating it for my amusement. But when I look up, he is peering into my face, frowning as if he could tell I was trying to remember how he sounds when he says the word "hello," and the words "Susan" and "Carolyn," words he would have said as soon as he saw them.

When he has gone off to feed the chickens, I go upstairs and climb over the balcony and across the porch roof. While I sit in the old Chinese elm tree with my arms wrapped around it, I can hear him clucking to the chickens as he takes the eggs from beneath them. High up in a tree so ancient my mother thinks every winter will be its last, the word "green," a word I've heard my grandfather say all my life—a word he has exclaimed in the spring about the first blade of grass, a word he has carried into the house with a basket of new peas from his garden, a word that formerly was part of a place I liked to visit— that word "green" has shriveled into something so small and hard, even its meaning has been altered.

Coming back down the sidewalk, he looks smaller than I've ever noticed. When he passes beneath the tree, I look down at the top of his hat and into his speckled bucket half-filled with brown, warm eggs. I think if I'm quiet he won't see me high up inside the leaf-filled branches. But he stops and looks up.

I know he sees me, but I look straight out through the branches to the mountains and the sky beyond them. I study a bare stretch where Sweet's Lumber Company has cut a section of trees like a deep gouge into the mountain. When a long time has passed, or what seems like a long time to me, I hear his shoes scuffing against the sidewalk. The screen door opens and whispers back into place. The kitchen door clunks closed behind him.

In the tree, the buds of leaves around me are closed so tightly on themselves, I think my mother may be right. This year they won't open.

When I've lain in bed so long I think my mother may already be asleep, I ask a question I already know the answer to.

"Does Granddad have an accent?" I say to the ceiling above me, and for a long time, my mother doesn't answer. I hear her turn from her side to her back. I think we're both looking at the scraggly crack in the ceiling, visible only at night when the street light casts its yellow beam upon it.

When she speaks, her words go straight up and are swallowed by that. "I suppose he has," she says quietly. "German. Though I've never noticed."

In the silence, I think she's listening, trying to hear the sound of my grandfather's voice. And then she turns and faces the window. In the dark, her head and the pillow are a grey hump against the faint light beyond it.

"Do I have one?" I whisper so quietly, I think she may not be able to hear me.

"No," she says after a long time, but there's a question in her voice as if she's considering whether the way people speak is something we could catch from them, like a disease, before we even know they have it.

In the darkness, I blame Susan Pendleton for everything. I think she has turned my grandfather into someone he hadn't been before she made fun of him. If it weren't for her, he'd still be going around talking about green things and the land they grew from, and no one would think anything was strange about it.

And then I remember that on the playground, all the girls were giggling. Every girl who heard Susan mutilate the word "Greenland" had recognized my grandfather's voice as soon as she said it.

I see something even more disturbing. If my grandfather has always pronounced his words differently from everyone else, something must be wrong with my family, an inherent, genetic sort of deafness that won't permit us to hear what we don't want to be hearing. I think we may have a problem with our vision as well, a kind of blindness that transforms what looks strange to everyone else into something that appears perfectly normal to us.

I think that the whole time we were planning our trip to Alaska, everyone else may have known we weren't really going. I can't think of one other mother who would consider loading her children into a car and driving them off to Alaska by herself, or who would plan such a fantasy with them as if it could actually happen.

In the morning, I go down the outside stairway alone. From the front seat of my mother's old gray Plymouth, I watch my brothers come out of my grandparents' part of the house, banging their suitcases against the porch railing, hurrying and excited. Behind them, my mother is calling good-bye over her shoulder. My grandfather is coming down the steps with her brown suitcase in his hand. In the open screen door behind him, my grandmother is in her pink chenille bathrobe, waving her handkerchief in my direction.

While the rest of them are coming down the sidewalk, headed toward the car, I sit with my eyes down over a stack of comic books I intend to read the whole time we travel.

And then my mother is in the car and the motor is running. Behind the steering wheel, her face is set straight ahead as if she were already searching for my aunt's face at her dining room window, grasping the steering wheel as if it were a rope she'd have to use to pull the car from Mayesville to Greenland.

My grandfather's hand is resting on the sill of my open window. He is leaning down so he can see inside the car, his gray eyes set soberly on mine.

"You'll have a fine time," he says before he steps back. At the edge of the yard where lilac bushes lean over the fence, pressing their purple flowers all around him, his face lifts suddenly as if he'd just seen something that explained my silence.

"This year Greenland," he calls to me. "Next year Alaska." And then his hand is whopping the side of the car, urging us forward as if the old Plymouth were a horse on which all of us were mounted and we were galloping off toward pastures far more interesting and distant than where we were going.

In the back seat, my brothers are shouting "giddyap" as if they held reins in their hands. My mother is smiling, her eyes excited as a child's.

"I wish you'd stop your pouting," she says, but it's more than that. All the way up Wolf Creek Pass and through the San Luis Valley, I sit sideways, my face toward the window. Beside me, grasses and trees and fence posts streak past so close I think if I put my hand out, I could touch them. The grader ditch is a blue road itself whizzing at breakneck speed in the opposite direction. But when I look up and beyond those things, the distant hills and mountains are motionless like great solemn beings watching us go past. Inside the car, my mother's eyes are locked on the road ahead as if it were all that existed, but I think we are going nowhere. All day we will travel, for weeks and weeks we might travel; but when the car stops and we get out of it we will be right back where we started.

Only one thing is different: something has broken off like a splinter far down inside me—a long thin sliver of wood so delicate I won't be able to get it out in one piece no matter how carefully I work to remove it.

"Tye Bop II"
JOHN TOMS
(pastel on paper)

Music for the Gods
James Gurley

—after the Sheridan and Bruce Fahnestock
South Sea Expedition recordings, Indonesia, 1941—

The music enters me, opens me up to a world
where a rooster crows and a gong calls
to the heavens, the Bali gamelan players

asking the benevolent spirits to possess
the masked dancers, their bodies, the glorious
music, a spatial exaltation in each step,

each gift of incense or flowers. Or maybe I
only imagine this. The temple, the three-ness
interwoven in the wooden mallets striking into

the dancer's ecstasy, the unexpected shifts in key
as the gods descend. Maybe it's something else
the Fahnestocks capture on their scratchy disks,

the players not aware what the microphone is for.
After his brother died during the war,
Sheridan stored these recordings in his attic.

For him that world had vanished with its harmony
or reason, the vast chords that unite us,
where he watches dancers approach as sacred beasts.

What happens to these voices that beautify the land?
The field song, the songs of worship?
This holy fragrance begins with the xylophone,

the long-drawn-out chant of women's voices.
And stays with me in the passion for music itself,
the rhythmic almost involuntary flexing

of my friend Art Liestman's hands testing a new drum
he has made for pitch. Wedging the curved barrel
between his thighs, he hits the flat surface

and feels the drum resonate through his body.
This improvised passage marks a lull in his telling
me how the drum was built, and how the wood bound

inside the metal frame adhered to its new shape,
pressing against the looping strands of wire.
He plays a random melody. Music rises from

a hollowed-out channel inside the wood, its voice dark
and harmonic. Around us the half-finished slats
of wood, the table saw and metal hoops.

All his life he's loved the richness of sounds,
of voices in jazz groups, in women singers,
where the song overcomes a silly broken heart,

even the loss of faith. Neither of us can resist
the drum, our body wholly taken by its summons.
We beat out a passable tune, share this music,

how it enters our bodies no matter what instrument
we chose. Maybe that's what the Fahnestocks capture,
not the Bali rituals or trance songs but this

high-pitched world they witness in the gamelan players,
their droning cadences like the steady rhythm
of our blood that goes unnoticed.

The dancers gyrating slowly, but never stopping,
while the Fahnestock brothers give us
the illusion, the temple music the gods inhabit.

White
Renée Ashley

TEENS CHARGED IN SWAN'S DEATH

...The youths grabbed the bird when he came to
the defense of his mate, held him down, stabbed
him, and cut off his head with a hunting knife....
—*The Rockland Journal News*,
May 4, 1994

Trespass. And the bright stars
    deep behind the willows: those boys

    in their sallow skins vaulting
the low fence, shortcutting

the path—cool midnight
    and the nacre of moonlight

    around them—then fear
a white thing beating: the breadth

of a pond alone in the span, the white
    hiss, the gates of those mad hearts

    slamming. That much fast light—
how quickly the knife must

have cut. It is important
    to believe this: what else

    could they do but sever
what moved with such white speed,

with so much fire that it burned
    that brightly? What else

    is our fear but a white thing
lunging, what is memory but

some furious white hissing our
    names? Everything

moves quickly in moonlight:
no matter what we cross over,

no matter how we close these beaten
hearts, we live our endless

lives with one white cry,
with the dazzling, indelible shame.

Severe
Renée Ashley

Not the way the old man
sent the children flying:

not with a boot or a rock,
not with a string of hot

curses, no, the blue
fled the sky in a general

way, a tenuous lessening
of blue, a toning down.

The way outside my window
the whole branch with its

glorious bracts lifted
as though the wind had

gentle hands. And then
the storm like a drunken fist:

the way the curve of the great swale
buckled in the flash and the dogwood

fell. That fast. Severe. The way it
shimmered in the catastrophic light.

Mobile
Sarah Browning

I don't often use car metaphors
in poems
being a girl.
But when I got stuck in fifth gear
on Route 2, racing to Boston,
it was irresistible.
I need my linkages lubricated,
the shy garage man told me
and he's right.
I need to feel the connections
in my life slide
and slip more gracefully.

Built to Last
Sarah Browning

I've read there's no such
thing as prairie any more,
that topsoil rich and luminous
is dumping and scuttling deep
into the Mississippi,
that flood walls
reach high on the delta plain.

Here's a shopping cart on the horizon.
A small white child has pushed it
clattering across the dirty driveway—
that paved and cracked landscape of the middle.
Here's a spotted quilt with pee, railing-draped.

To be swallowed there in the middle
of the country, walking forever on the flat earth,
the history of the land's betrayal
pounding up through my feet.

If we dump the earth quickly into the sea
I want to know if we are left in neutral,
a wash of three inches,
a netherland of swamp with the moon always pale
and present above us.

Here's a tree marked by our insistence,
letters scrawled in the beechy-smooth trunk.
Many ways to make our mark.

Revolutions
Florin Ion Firimita

REVOLUTION: "1. a complete and forcible overthrow of an established government
or political system...6a. A turning round or rotating, as on an axis."
Webster Encyclopedic Unabridged Dictionary of the English Language

"Yet you and I are not afraid here," said Levanter.
"We are not." said Woytek, "because we've known greater fear in other places."
Jerzy Kosinski—*Blind Date*

I stepped on Lenin's face—his picture was splashed with drops of
December mud, but he was still looking at me, not seeming to care. We were
caught by the dance, a ritual dance of people who never met before, now linked
by this collective silent movement. It was our local Eastern European
Woodstock, our Mardi Gras with tanks, mud and dance and Lenin's picture
flapping up and down in the air, torn from the red bonded books thrown out of
the windows of the Central Committee Communist Party headquarters.

They said it was a revolution, but what did that really mean? For a few
days, we were a country without leaders. The streets remained unswept and
covered with small pieces of paper. I hugged people whom I hadn't met before
or since, and I did not go to work because I had a few friends to bury. Was that
the long-awaited freedom? Was it that now you could find a grocery store open
late at night like in the West and not freeze when you took a shower after work,
or was it that we were now able to scribble slogans on the walls without being
afraid, or more correctly, without remembering what fear was? Was it that now,
after forty-five years of Communism, we were finally learning to die for
something? And was it worth it? What guarantees was freedom bringing? Was
it the freedom of judging someone without a trial, like that soldier who I saw on
my street, whose head was chopped off and propped up on the top of a burned-
out armored vehicle with a cigarette sticking out of his dark-blue lips? Or was
it the macabre joy of an old man urinating on the burned body of an assumed
terrorist on the sidewalk where I used to stroll at night trying to impress my
dates by reciting long, laboriously memorized passages from Rilke? Who cared
about Rilke now? Poets never made good revolutionaries. They were just naive
Christs of the pen who once in a while made good martyrs.

The street's asphalt was engraved from the blades of the tanks. I
remembered my mother's tales from World War II, when the windows of her
parents' house trembled from the same type of tanks which now passed by;
forty years earlier, in the same city, she hid in the basement, afraid of being
raped by the Russian soldiers.

Now the asphalt had the roughness of an alligator's skin, with deep, sharp wounds in it, like someone had tried to kill the street itself. I stopped and touched the lacerated ground. Rilke's verses—no one's verses—were to be found there. The corpse on my street had stayed there for a few days. You could not recognize anything human in it anymore except the boots. Someone said that it was the body of the traitor. Then, I saw the old man's face, the mute, irradiant satisfaction, after waiting so many painful years, a revenge so simple to carry out, his own private revolution, unzipping the fly of his stained pants like the trigger of a gun.

They said that this is what revolutions looked like, and there I was in the middle of it, with a Mozart record under my arm and a pound of goat cheese bought under the table from a friend, and suddenly nothing made sense anymore. It was not the fact that the special troops could have shown up anytime and beaten or even killed us, but it was the deadly silence of the city that frightened me that day. A city of two million mute people, a city that suddenly seemed immersed in a huge fish tank, inhabited with wax statues, while cars went into hiding or became extinct, and hypnotized crowds were waiting to be abducted by an alien force. We were living in a time bomb.

But it was so uncommonly good that people could actually now look at each other. We had been in a hurry all the time, rarely looking in each other's eyes; for years we learned how to recognize the empty looks on the faces of the secret police agents strolling the streets; we learned how to avoid each other. All this time, we were individual walking cells without keys to our locks. Now, though, it seemed different.

I spotted a chef outside his restaurant gazing toward the plaza, and I smiled looking at his tall, impeccable cap; he confidently smiled back, like we were all in this, and there was no going back. There was a blue and white police car in front of us and about ten or fifteen young and scared policemen trying to hide their AK-47s. The car started to drive in circles, circles of fear. (Someone said, that car seems to be a very nervous car, and people laughed, an uneasy laughter, breaking the fear. Laughter does that.) You could see how the young officers would rather have been naked in the middle of that crowd than wearing those pale blue uniforms, totally deprived of their authority.

Two students started shouting and someone brought a red flag, the sickle and the hammer like a headache in the middle. Someone else pulled out a lighter and the cloth was instantly caught by a yellow fire, and people started dancing. It was so easy. Why didn't we do it earlier? It was like the thrill of opening new routes on winter-closed paths in the Carpathians during cold full-moon nights, when I would pack my rucksack and climb to my friend's chalet. With the wolves always in the background, always waiting, it was then that I learned how to gamble with death. It was the same type of danger. It also reminded me of the quiver I felt seeing the naked outline of my eighth grade math teacher's body, revealing itself beneath her sheer clothing every time she walked through the powerful sunlight coming from one of the tall classroom windows. I was unable to focus on numbers, preferring to stare at her. It was a passport to hell, like getting drunk and playing Russian roulette. It was like the winter afternoon when I furiously resigned from one of my odd jobs and started drawing an old oak tree in a middle of a park until my fingers froze on the cold, black charcoal. It was like the night that I fell in love for the first time, or when I closed my eyes and parachuted from a plane above the green fields of Transylvania.

What they called revolution was a mixture of hidden lust, idealism and dance, the wolf in me that needed both to pray and throw up. After all, the old man urinating on the dead soldier was performing an ancient ritual that combined all these aspects. Me kissing an unknown woman in the middle of fifty thousand people, a woman whose name I didn't even know, ready to make love with her right there, on the wet and black macadam because I was happy and because I was afraid to die; the student writing with a piece of chalk on the walls of the university until his whitened fingers started bleeding; other students burning the red flag and dancing around its ashes; me stomping on Lenin's face (how far were we from the tribe shrinking the heads of their enemies and displaying them as trophies?) The mob cheering at the view of Marie-Antoinette stepping towards the guillotine; two centuries later, the smiling people in their clean suits outside their offices in downtown Bucharest, still thinking that this was a civilized century and revolutions could happen without blood, after you signed out on your office time card and go for a pizza and a glass of red wine with your friends. We were all performing the same ancient ritual.

But the barefoot children walking with large white candles in their hands, an army of Joan D'Arcs against the tanks on the other side like big, gray, metal elephants, the silence before death, proved that this this was not a civilized century.

For a very short while we ignored any religion and any morals; we were above both, as naive as Adam and Eve walking around naked in the Garden of Eden, before the laws, ready to accept anything, not knowing we were naked and vulnerable, blind and happy. There is a cruelty in happiness and youth, and it was in the air like a shell, ready to explode. Standing there in the middle of the silent crowd, my mind was dancing, making large circles around the plaza, and my soul was holding hands with everyone. Happiness was bordering death.

I saw an acquaintance, a former classmate whom I had deliberately ignored over the years. In a moment I was next to him, my arm around his. We shook hands like two good friends, and it was so normal, I didn't even remember that only a week before I wasn't even able to sit with him in the same room. Then I saw other people who had seemed to have disappeared forever from my life; how did they end up there, in the middle of all that, as if in a huge family reunion? If my parents, dead for a while, had shown up, I would not have been surprised. If you want to meet people whom you have lost for a long time, find yourself a revolution.

We went to the revolution like going to an experimental play performed on one of those circular stages where you can watch and be watched, where you can write your own script and act. We were the actors and we were the spectators. We built the stage, but we also paid for the tickets. It is not surprising that Communist countries produce remarkable actors. History was sitting somewhere in the balcony, waiting for bodies and for blood worth mentioning in college textbooks and Ph.D. dissertations, but we drank champagne and cared about soccer, rock'n'roll and passports. And it was so sunny that December that I thought that vendors would start distributing fresh, cold drinks among those people with wounded looks and bandaged souls. I was thirsty and I was hungry, and I loved my thirst and my hunger: they became my pets and my companions. People's unshaven faces, their empty stomachs, Mozart, goat cheese and Lenin. This was history, so banal and unheroic that Mr. Malraux would have laughed and painted the whole thing over in a more statuesque manner.

The air had some sort of gray powder in it, just like after my first Fourth of July in America one year later. One of my friends blew up hundreds of fireworks in her backyard while I sat on a chaise lounge, sipping a Manhattan, chatting with a blonde lawyer from Miami. She suddenly asked me if I could fire a few of her "bombs." I said no, thank you, I'll skip it this year. It had reminded me of the skies of Bucharest that warm December, with the trajectories of the colored bullets above my head and the whisper of death in my ear. The dance started in Romania was ending there, full circle, with the images of pain so close to the images of the cool pleasure from my drink.

Bucharest was a ruined city. During the years, demolished churches were replaced by impersonal cement block houses. Entire streets were wiped out by the government bulldozers. In Communist ideology, the past had to be completely erased, making room for a new history to be written. But that December afternoon, Bucharest had suddenly regained its lost mystery. Because of the mystical magnetism of the day, I expected every door of every house to be open and to find large bowls of fresh fruit waiting for us on every table. I closed my eyes, imagining dew drops on the skin of red apples, the smell of oranges and green melons. It was getting late and I was hungry; I reached into my pocket and found a handful of bank notes; I remembered that it was payday.

I found my way through the waiting crowd, and went to buy some bread. A bakery was open, and everyone was eating warm bread and drinking champagne. It was the only drink you could buy in Bucharest; there were rumors that the water was poisoned, so everyone had an excuse to get drunk. I was not used to that kind of lighted store in the middle of the city. Usually Bucharest was covered in darkness every night, with dark street lights and no colorful neon signs. After all, there was nothing to advertise. I bought a few loaves of bread and jars of peach preserves. We brought everything back to the plaza and gave people fresh, warm bread which they dipped into the juice. Freedom was good and it had a taste of preserved orchards and homey flour; we took bites of it with our eyes closed, like making love or listening to music. Pamplona moved to Bucharest and we were waiting for the invisible bulls of the night to show up.

It was only six p.m. and we looked forward to the rest of the celebration. But with shattering explosions of guns, it ended. Smiles changed into grimaces of pain within a second, and I could not read those faces anymore. We were out of Eden, stepping on the fresh bread, mixing it under our steps with mud and blood. (I had the same feeling a year later, when walking on via XX Settembre in Rome as a new immigrant, I entered the church of Santa Maria della Vittoria. Bernini's Saint Theresa greeted me with the same hidden duality in her smile; the mystic ecstasy was dangerously close to the sexual ecstasy, pleasure, just an inch from pain.) That night in Bucharest the faces displayed no borders between death and joy, until that first bullet dissolved the magic. We became bodies again, vulnerable, miserable, hunted bodies, followed from every building through the scopes of the infrared sighted rifles of our assassins. The hunters and the hunted were equally swallowed by the night, and curiously, we suddenly remembered God. I let go of the hand of the woman next to me. I didn't need her anymore. My palms were suddenly sweaty. That collective soul vanished quickly and was replaced by real, almost touchable cries. We regained our fragile individualities again, becoming, once more, confused bodies, dead bodies being stepped on, poor matter juggled around by History.

I was running with the Mozart record under my arm, *Dances and Minuets*, it said on the cover, and yes, I was dancing on the highwire of the History; why did I let the woman's hand slip out of mine? Why did I keep the record? I don't know. Mozart did not help me accommodate the feeling of stepping on human flesh, like on a confused sea with wounded waves, ready to sink into its own depth. From this perspective, Mozart was no better than Lenin. We acknowledged ourselves and only ourselves, the touchable and visible selves and nothing more. When violence started, culture ceased to exist.

If it weren't for the dead bodies, this could have been a Christmas night, I thought. I guess that we all longed for real fireworks. And in the middle of all that, I stopped and closed my eyes, wishing to dissolve into the night. I was tired of surviving and I wanted to close the circle. I stopped. I couldn't hear the cries anymore, not even the bullets flying around my ear or the people screaming and pushing me around. Then, I touched my face; it was rough and unshaven; this wasn't the face that I wanted to die with. Give me a chance, I thought, but my thought was flat and tired. Just one more chance.

And they ceased fire.

II

"BUCHAREST, Dec. 25 (Reuter) Sympathizers and those nostalgic for the certainties of Communism held a Christmas Day vigil at the grave of Romanian dictator Nicolae Ceausescu, executed by firing squad five years ago on Sunday."

"Good to see you, Mike." I had said a few evenings earlier when I saw him jumping into his blue car. I didn't get a chance to see him too often, for as an officer he was always on a mission somewhere, and we only met weekends on top of the mountain or at his house. We were helping out our friends from the rescue team, searching for lost skiers and hikers on the vast plateau of the Bucegi mountains.

Last time we were at the chalet, the snow was so white that it seemed almost colored, and red and blue accents were left under the sinking light of the sunset. We found a guy walking around in his hat and trench coat against the sixty-mile-per-hour wind; he was almost frozen when we brought him inside. There were few people inside, skis and rucksacks all over, and the wind was pounding at the doors. It was Sunday and I hoped that the funicular railway would cease operating and I could have an excuse for skipping a day of work. I wanted to stay there, buried in snow. Then Mike went and called his wife.

Magda didn't join him that winter, and we all missed her presence, the long, dark hair and the broad smile on her face behind the John Lennon sunglasses. She had to stop her trips and interrupt her law studies for a while; she was pregnant.

"It's a good hobby," I heard Mike say when he came back. "Saving people's lives."

"You mean." I said, "we're not here to meet women?"

It was true, during the years we had a good time and many successful rescues, but we partied a lot as well. There were also times when we arrived too late. That December we found someone frozen on the top of the mountain. His girlfriend had rejected his marriage proposal, so he drank half a bottle of Polish vodka and fell asleep under a rock. When we found him, the bottle was laying empty in the snow, the metal of his watchband deeply embedded in his wrist. He was dead. Mike started slapping the corpse with one of his skis and pounding it with his fists, and for the first and only time I saw him crying. I never saw him so furious.

"You son-of-a-bitch," he said. "You stupid son-of-a-bitch."

From his car he gave me the victory sign the day the Revolution started.

"Merry Christmas!" I waved the bottle of red wine that I brought with me. "Thirsty?"

He was on vacation and could have stayed home, but he was one of those who didn't like watching revolutions on TV.

"Yes. Save me a glass for later."

I stayed with Magda for a few hours. We watched the revolution like a soap opera on their black-and-white TV until she couldn't take it anymore. I guess she was nervous about him leaving like that to lead his tank unit, so we watched their wedding videos. They had been married for only ten months after exchanging rings in the front of the Heroes Monument. It was a soldier thing; she hadn't liked it too much, but she loved him and respected his decisions.

Soon I had to go, too. A magnet was pulling me downtown, towards that bizarre Christmas with deadly fireworks; they were still shooting from every roof, and I hoped that I could reach home. Armored vehicles competed with people for the street, windows were smashed and public phones did not work. From the top of the buildings, invisible terrorists proved their existence. It was like the night itself was shooting at us.

Late in the morning I arrived home. The power and water were off and in the refrigerator I found only a bottle of champagne and a loaf of bread. The ghost of my Christmas tree governed the living room. I ate the bread and drank a glass of champagne before collapsing into a dreamless sleep on the cold kitchen floor.

III

I jumped on the opened platform of the truck. There were people with flags around me and someone had an AK-47 pointed outside. It was raining and the procession following us on foot looked like a sad reptile waving its tail in the mud. The cemetery was on the outskirts of the city, and when we arrived, I spotted men with rifles at the edges of all the surrounding buildings. Most of the fights were over, but they were there to protect us, just in case, defending death with death.

Mike was laying there in a brand new gray suit (Why do we dress up when we die?) His face was blue and his hands were crossed on his chest, with his wedding ring shining on his ring finger. He looked strange. I was used to him more in a red ski outfit, in his hiking boots with ski glasses hanging on his chest. The soldiers gave him military honors and some people embraced him for the last time. Then we left under the cloudy sky, and that evening I had a long chat with God.

"I saw it all on TV," an American friend awkwardly told me two years later; actually, even in those days in Bucharest, some people chose to be in front of their TV, while others met with bullets on the deadly streets. It was a matter of opinion. Who was right, those who waited for History to happen without them, or those who naively thought they were making History? How naive of Mr. Malraux, some forty years earlier, believing that Man makes History and not the other way around. From a distance of six thousand miles, in her comfortable house in Santa Monica, my friend was sipping a large soda, surfing the channels while I was on my knees, feeling the octopus-like wetness of the mud, waiting for the Bullet. Actor or spectator, who was right? History, in the balcony, was laughing at both of us: only History has the remote control.

It was a long time before Magda showed me Mike's bullet-proof helmet with traces of sweat around its inner leather edges and the perfect round bullet hole. The night he died, he was able to phone her somehow and kept asking her to prepare the gray suit for his funeral. She laughed at him, but he felt death coming toward him. She didn't want to believe. Of course she didn't.

That Christmas night, she gave birth to an eight-pound boy. She named him Mike. A few years later, he learned that his father died around the time he was born.

Critics say that few things changed in Romania, and that the country went back to its dark days by choosing Revolution over Evolution. I am optimistic, but there are certain truths that cannot be denied. The old guard formed a new guard of businessmen and the government has proved incapable of governing so far. Crime went up and shameless corruption is officially tolerated. Only a few were charged with the December massacres and, six years later, the invisible "terrorists" remain invisible. Romanians now have their own kind of JFK conspiracy to figure out while a few still crave the false security of the old days. Between 1945 and 1989, about one and a half million innocent Romanians were thrown in political prisons. More than five hundred thousand died there. Most of those responsible for the genocide are now enjoying the benefits of a serene retirement. In Eastern Europe, History is still playing macabre tricks.

Sometimes I wish I had Mike's helmet here with me; often I dream about it, a khaki flower pot on my window sill in which I would grow fresh tulips. I remember him every time I take a long weekend and go skiing in Vermont. But all I can do is put a glass of Romanian red wine every Christmas night on my kitchen table, and wait, just in case he is still thirsty.

About the Artist

JOHN TOMS is a Denver artist whose work is displayed widely throughout the nation, including at the Denver Black Arts Festival. The featured pieces are from his acclaimed Jazz Series. The cover piece, also from his Jazz Series, is called "Tye Bop I." The DuSable Museum in Chicago recently purchased an original piece from this series. Some of his pieces are available in limited-edition offset lithograph prints. For further information on obtaining prints, please contact Black Market Ink at 969 Mt. Airy Drive, SW, Atlanta, GA 30311, or call 1-800-264-1178.

About the Contributors

HOMERO ARIDJIS is one of Mexico's leading literary and political figures. Honored for both his poetry and his fiction, Aridjis is also the president of Group 100, Mexico's international ecopolitical leadership organization. He has been active in the rescue of sea turtles, among many other animals. He is the author of *Time of the Angels*, *Los ojos desoblados* and *Antologia poética 1960-1994*, among many other books.

RENÉE ASHLEY's collection, *SALT*, won the Brittingham Prize in Poetry (University of Wisconsin Press, 1991). She has been twice awarded the Kenyon Review Award for Literary Excellence; she's been awarded the Open Voice Award in Poetry, and the Ruth Lake Memorial and Robert H. Winner Awards from the Poetry Society of America, and the 1996 Chelsea Prize in Poetry. Her work appears in *Kenyon Review*, *New England Review*, *American Voice*, *Poetry*, and other journals. She teaches creative writing in New Jersey and New York.

"'White' was the result of an assignment I gave an advanced poetry workshop. We had read Brigit Pegeen Kelly's breathtaking poem 'Dead Doe,' from her book *Song*, and had discussed the myriad pitfalls possible in writing about dead animals. Kelly had fallen into none, we decided. The next week one of the participants brought in the article about the swan from a local paper. We decided, lightheartedly and without much hope, to write from the act described in the article with as much dignity and restraint as possible without borrowing directly from Kelly's technique. The poems that came in the next week, I must confess, were very, very good. All of us were surprised. We never did, though, write a thank you to Brigit Kelly. 'Severe' is one of the few poems in my work that actually came from staring out a window—though I certainly hope it doesn't sound like an all-too-familiar staring-out-the-window poem! It was a bad storm, hurricane strength, and we lost our magnificent dogwood beneath what seemed to be the weight of the sound of the thunder. I was heartsick. The poem, I guess, is an elegy or a complaint. Or a plea."

KAREN AUVINEN lives in Colorado where she is an Artist-in-Residence in Writing and Storytelling. She received her M.A. in Creative Writing from CU-Boulder, where her poetry manuscript, *Flesh Remembrances*, won the 1994 Harcourt Brace Jovanovich Award. Her poems and stories have most recently appeared in *Fireweed*, *Alligator Juniper*, *SniperLogic* and *the literary hotgirls review*.

"I was thinking about desire when I wrote this story—the architectonics of it. I think the experience of it can be quite shaking in a way that can rearrange one's physiology. Also, writing is essentially an act of desire, so that gets mixed into the soup as well."

DARRELL BOURQUE is a Cajun poet living in Lafayette, Louisiana. He teaches writing at the University of Southern Louisiana, where he also coordinates the yearly Deep South Writer's Conference. His most recent book is *Plainsongs*.

SARAH BROWNING is director of Amherst Writers & Artists Institute, an organization providing creative writing workshops for low-income women and their children. Her poems are forthcoming or have appeared in such journals as *The New York Quarterly*, *Mudfish*, *The Seattle Review*, *The Midwest Quarterly*, *Sycamore Review*, and *Peregrine*. One was nominated for a Pushcart Prize.

"Sharon Olds wrote in a poem about Muriel Rukeyser's act of solidarity with a jailed Korean poet: 'Pass it on: a poet, a woman,/ a witness, standing.' This is what we can hope for, I suppose—to be witnesses in our poetry to this awful century, to record what we can of the truth."

BOBBY BYRD lives in El Paso, Texas. A poet and writer, he also teaches at the University of Texas at El Paso. He is the publisher and editor of Conco Puntos Press. He is the author of *On the Transmigration of Souls in El Paso.*

DINA COE After many years of working as a flight attendant for a well-known international airline that bit the dust, Dina Coe finds herself teaching composition and literature courses at various local colleges and universities. Through both jobs, she has continued writing poems, and now has two volumes ready for publication, titled *Travels at Dusk* and *Reader in Pandemonium.* She lives in a rural setting in central New Jersey.

"'Avalanche Trail' is one of a group of poems written after spending a vacation in Wyoming and Montana; in the case of this poem, Glacier Park. What struck me was the lush and rugged unfamiliarity of the Montana landscape, further elaborated by the unexpectedness of a rain forest in glacier mountains, and this sense of strangeness with its allure and its difficulties doubled by being in the presence of a new love.

MATTHEW COOPERMAN's poems have appeared in *Mid-American Review, Chicago Review, Bombay Gin,* and *Field.* His new work is forthcoming in *Denver Quarterly* and *Tampa Review.* Cooperman is the editor of *Quarter after Eight,* a journal of prose and commentary.

MICHAEL DORSEY's fiction has appeared in *Allegheny Review, Another Chicago Magazine,* and other magazines. "No Man's Land" is part of a collection entitled *Between Dreams,* which he hopes to see published someday.

FLORIN ION FIRIMITA is a thirty-year-old Romanian-born artist who lives with his cat, Matisse, in a serene Connecticut village. He paints and writes almost every day, away from any disturbing revolutions.

"I like to consider myself mainly a visual artist, and I believe that writing saves my paintings from being too narrative. On the other hand, I think that being a painter helps me visualize my stories. After emigrating to the U.S. four years ago, I started learning English from late-night talk shows and hours of heavy reading, from Hemingway and Durrell to supermarket tabloids. Almost immediately I abandoned my native language because I could not live or write comfortably in two languages. I used to believe that my years in Communist Romania were a waste of time; fear, tragedy, and despair followed me everywhere. Nothing good seemed to grow out of that. I had to break up with the past and come to American to be able to understand and interpret my experiences. What made me start writing, besides a need for sharing, was changing this role, from participant to observer. Today I realize that, even if I look at my stories mostly with an outsider's eye, I cannot avoid finding myself within them, patient and doctor, actor and spectator, at the same time."

JAMES GURLEY lives in Seattle, Washington, and has poems forthcoming or recently published in *Poetry, Poetry Northwest, Prism International* and *Switched-On Gutenberg* (http://weber.u.washington.edu/~jnh). In 1995 a chapbook of his poetry, *Transformations,* was published by Reference West. This poem is from a recently completed manuscript, *Temple of Science.*

KATE LYNN HIBBARD has an M.F.A. in Creative Writing from the University of Oregon. Her work has appeared in *Calyx, Seattle Review, New Letters*, and the anthology *Garden Variety Dykes* (Herbooks, 1994). She has worked as a teacher, fund-raiser; secretary, massage therapist, waitress, and frozen pizza assembler.

"'The Meaning of Romance' was indeed inspired by a good-bye kiss in an airport bathroom stall in Minneapolis. When I brought the poem to my workshop, I was told by one student that it was an unrealistic scenario, since all the gay people he knew were perfectly comfortable displaying affection in public. Well, good for them! Unfortunately, that hasn't been my experience, although I suppose the clandestine does offer more material for poetry...''

LAWSON FUSAO INADA's work has appeared in numerous publications, as well as being inscribed in stone along the Willamette River, and the inspiration for Composer Andrew Hill. His book, *Legends from the Camp*, is an incredible masterpiece of poetry. His poems have appeared in previous issues of *Many Mountains Moving*.

MARIE LEE's work has been published in *Kenyon Review, American Voice*, and Norton's *New Worlds of Literature*. She'll be a visiting lecturer at Yale next year.

"Part of this story was inspired by a Maine friend's recounting of introducing some land-locked Native American students to lobster. I have always thought lobsters look unappetizingly like giant cockroaches, and I guess the students sort of thought so, too."

GREGORY McNAMEE's most recent books are *Gila: The Life and Death of an American River* (Crown Publishers), *The Sierra Club Desert Reader* (Sierra Club Books) and, with Art Wolfe, *In the Presence of Wolves* (Crown Publishers). His literary and environmental journalism appears regularly in publications such as *Outside, The Nation, The Bloomsbury Review* and *Audubon*. McNamee lives in Tucson, Arizona. His work and translations have appeared in previous issues of *Many Mountains Moving*.

CHRISTINE L. MONAHAN was born in 1970, and is originally from Long Island, New York, where she lived until she was nineteen. As an undergraduate, she studied English and Art History at the University of Missouri-Columbia. She has a master's degree in Writing from the University of New Hampshire, where she studied fiction writing, and poetry under the instruction of Mekeel McBride. Her work has appeared in the anniversary edition of *New Hampshire Images, Long Islander; Walt's Corner*, and *Crazyhorse*. She lives in New Hampshire where she teaches writing at a local college, and is a correspondent reporter for the *Portsmouth Herald*.

"'Infinite Odyssey Just before Closing Time' was birthed, in part, from a journal activity initiated by Mekeel, in which we continually practiced drawing before we wrote, in order to 'see' the lives of images more attentively. My sketch of a beer bottle caused me to focus on the bits of foam floating in the liquid, and to think of the bottle's inner geography. This lead me to think of the internal geography of a serious drinker I know, and of his Homeric journey into dissipation. In 'Having Been Removed from You, I Am,' the intense feeling of loss during many types of human separation can be such that an individual begins to define his or her identity by that feeling. This poem attempts to articulate that. The last stanza of the poem is rooted, to some extent, in Michelangelo's belief that every block of marble inherently contains the form of a sculpture within it, and in order to emerge as a sculpture, that form needs only to be freed from the rest of the marble attached to it."

LINDA NOWLIN, born in the Oklahoma Arbuckle Mountains and raised in Kansas, now lives and paints and writes in Salt Lake City, Utah, with her husband and son. Her poems have been published in *Cimarron Review*, *Elk River Review*, and *New Republic*.

"'A Letter Home' started out as a way of expressing my interior life and was intended to be a kind of explanation to my family (as insufficient as that may be) and a way of articulating the way I 'hear' words and try to make sense of the world around me. 'Car Love' arose from playing around with the idea of autoeroticism and the need to make sense of one of my stepfathers, his presence in my life, and his separate existence in the garage."

ELIZABETH ONESS' stories have appeared in *The Hudson Review*, *O. Henry Prize Stories*, *The Chicago Tribune*, *Glimmer Train*, *Crazyhorse*, and other magazines.

"Almost anyone who has waitressed in New York City has worked alongside of people who have come to this country at great cost, as well as actors and actresses hoping to 'make it.' In most ways the predicaments of the two are very different, but the quality of yearning is similar."

LOWRY PEI is the director of the Writing Program at Simmons College in Boston. A long-time resident of Cambridge, Massachusetts, Pei has taught at Harvard and at the University of California, among others. His story, "The Cold Room," was included in the *1984 Best American Short Stories*. He is the author of the novel *Family Resemblances*.

PATRICK PRITCHETT regularly reviews books for the *American Book Review*, the *LA View* and the *Boulder Daily Camera*. His first book of poems, *Dark Matter, Luminous Forms*, is currently looking for a home.

JEFFREY C. ROBINSON is a professor of English at the University of Colorado-Boulder. His books include *The Walk: Notes on a Romantic Image* (University of Oklahoma Press, 1989) and *Romantic Presences: Living Images from the Age of Wordsworth and Shelley* (Station Hill Press, 1995), a book of essays about attempting to write criticism in poetry.

WILLIAM PITT ROOT's latest collection is *Trace Elements from a Running Kingdom* (Confluence Press, 1994). The selection of poems in this issue are from a forthcoming manuscript in search of a publisher. He teaches at Hunter College and lives in Tucson, Arizona, commuting weekly.

RICHARD RYAL was born in a falling New York zone, making his way first to the legendary Long Island Delta, then west and south until he ran out of money. He leads ritual drumming groups and edits for cash when not working on his children's books.

"Almost all my pieces are concerned with the distinctions and similarities that become clear at the border between any two realms—in this case, the frontier between expertise and mystery. The astronomer, like this poet, wants to leap beyond the skin line and become a living part of what he loves, which can't be contained by any lens."

DIXIE SALAZAR currently teaches writing at California State University—Fresno, and the Corcoran State Prison. She has been published in numerous magazines, and has a chapbook, *Hotel Fresno*, and a novel, *Limbo* (White Pine Press, 1985).

"'American Meltdown' is part of a series of poems in which I continue to explore my split heritage (Spanish from my father and Anglo-Mississippi, the Deep South from my mother. I think of it as split, as in split personality, since it seems to have brought together quite disparate elements for me to contend with. First there is the matter of identity, then acknowledgement, acceptance, and integration, all part of a process which writing helps facilitate. Perhaps it's a uniquely American experience (whatever that is)."

AMY SCATTERGOOD is a graduate of the Iowa Writers' Workshop and Yale Divinity School. Recent poems have appeared or are forthcoming in *The New Republic, Grand Street, Prairie Schooner, Denver Quarterly, New England Review, Greensboro Review, Southern Humanities Review, Atlanta Review, New Orleans Review, Urbanus,* and others. She lives in Los Angeles with her husband.

"'Dreams of Empire' was the product of a cross-country road trip, after Nebraska started duplicating itself and the cornfields took on bizarre supernatural qualities. I thought I'd never get out of Iowa (read this both ways). 'Akhmatova' is a more recent poem, part of a new book that deals with issues of censorship, secrecy, erasure and the suppression and rewiring of history. Sort of like elegies to police spies and Sappho scholars."

LISA RUSS SPAAR teaches creative writing and administers the M.F.A. Program in Creative Writing at the University of Virginia. She is Poetry Consultant for *Iris: A Journal About Women,* and has published two chapbooks, *Cellar* (Alderman Press, 1983) and *Blind Boy on Skates* (Trilobite/University of North Texas, 1987). Her poems have appeared or are forthcoming in *Poetry, The Virginia Quarterly Review, Shenandoah, Poetry East, Crazyhorse, Ploughshares,* and elsewhere, and in 1996 she received an Individual Artist's Award from the Virginia Commission for the Arts for her full-length manuscript, *Rapunzel's Clock.* She lives in Charlottesville, Virginia, with her husband, the bassist Peter Spaar, and their three children.

"'Suzannah, My Dear' is a birth-day poem that, I hope, takes its cadences and pulse, in part, from Thelonius Monk's beautiful composition 'Ruby, My Dear.' Living with a jazz bassist and with small children has opened me to the musics of other languages and of new language maker/users, and to the pleasures of integrating these musics into my poems."

ALISON STONE's poems have appeared in *Paris Review, Poetry, Ploughshares,* and a variety of other journals and anthologies. She was awarded *New York Quarterly*'s Madeline Sadin Award, and *Poetry*'s Frederick Boch Prize. Her first book, Persephone Returning, has been a finalist in a number of competitions and is currently seeking a publisher. She earns her living as a psychotherapist in New York city.

"'Stillborn' is for my cousin. Her baby died in the eighth month, but she had to go through the birth process anyway. Her description of the whole thing moved me so much, I needed to write this. 'The Book' is about the change process. As a therapist (and client), I'm constantly awed by the ability of people to heal and recreate their lives. 'Sea Song' is about those snippy, under-the-surface disappointments and rages that characterize so many relationships. 'In A Palace of Snow' began about love in the time of AIDS, with a line I cut out, 'Darling, let's cheat death together.' Love between men and women does cheat death in a sense, because it frees us from the cartoon stereotypes (ice maiden, heartless warrior, etc.) we're conditioned to become. 'And it was Morning...' was a gift from the Goddess of poetry. It came to me 'out of nowhere' in its completed form, and when I read the words, it was like seeing them for the first time."

SYLVIA MULLEN TOHILL, originally from Colorado, completed her M.A. in creative writing at Kansas State University and now lives in Oregon where she writes fiction and teaches part-time at a community college. Her fiction has previously appeared in *South Dakota Review* and *Kansas Quarterly* and has won several awards, including the first place Graduate Fiction Award, a Seaton Award, and more recently a Pacific Northwest Writer's Award for literary short fiction. She is currently at work on a novel, *CRAZYCORA*, about a character who first came to life in one of the Mayesville stories.

"I grew up in a small town in southwest Colorado and traveled each summer to visit my cousins who lived in Greenland, a small farming community in eastern Colorado, but unlike the young narrator in my story, I never grew tired of those visits. 'Greenland,' one of twelve stories set in the fictional Mayesville, Colorado, began with an actual place, an actual moment, an actual person. In remembering the old two story house where I grew up, I saw my mother standing again beside the dining room table, a sack of groceries in her arms, transfixed by something far beyond what she could see through the window. On her face was an expression so filled with longing—an expression so clearly 'not of that place'—that seeing it now as a writer, I had to know where she'd gone and what happened when she came back. What I discovered, of course, was that once we've begun to travel, one road joins another and we often end up in unexpected places, the greatest journeys taking us back to ourselves, altered by what we've seen."

PAMELA USCHUK's work has been published in *Poetry Magazine, Parnassus Review, High Plains Literary Review*, and *Nimrod*. She was awarded the 1996 Ronald H. Bayes Award. Uschuk teaches poetry workshops on the Yaqui and Tohono O'odham reservations through Arts Reach and teaches writing at the Writing Center at the University of Arizona.

LATHA VISWANATHAN is a freelance copywriter working on her first collection of short stories. In 1994, she won the John Hazard Wildman Prize for fiction given by Louisiana State University. Her stories have appeared in *Mangrove Magazine* and *Fiction International*. She lives in Baton Rouge, Louisiana.

"Reading research material on elephants some years back, I came across an article that mentioned something about methane gas experiments carried out at the Guruvayur temple in South India. Need I say more?"

INGRID WENDT is the author of *Moving the House* (Boa) and *Singing the Mozart Requiem* (Breitenbush) and has been the recipient of the Juniper Prize for poetry. Her work has appeared in numerous journals and anthologies.

CAROLYN BEARD WHITLOW, Associate Professor of English and Chairperson of the African American Studies Concentration at Guilford College in Greensboro, North Carolina, teaches creative writing and African American literature. A New Formalist, she earned her M.F.A. from Brown University, and was a finalist for the 1991 Barnard New Women Poets Prize. Her poems have appeared in *Callaloo* and *Kenyon Review*, among others. Lost Roads published her first poetry collection, *Wild Meat*, in 1986 and her poems have been anthologized in *A Formal Feeling Comes: Poems in Form by Contemporary Women* (Story Line Press, 1994). Her recent work, poems from her manuscript, *Mean Blue*, will appear in *Mockingbird* and *Crab Orchard Review*.

Many Mountains Moving, Inc. is a 501(c)(3) nonprofit organization. If you work for an institution or organization that supports literature and the arts and may wish to make a tax-deductible donation, or know of any individuals who may wish to make a contribution, please ask them to contact us at Many Mountains Moving, 420 22nd St., Boulder, CO 80302. Phone (303)545-9942. Fax (303)444-6510.

The editors wish to
congratulate the winners of our first annual

Many Mountains Moving Literary Awards.

FICTION

Michael Ramos
"When the Soldier Sleeps in the Field"

ESSAY

Leonard Chang
"Sweets Etcetera"

POETRY

Sarah Wolbach
"Bathing Susan"

HONORABLE MENTION FOR POETRY

Naomi Shihab Nye
"Muchas Gracias por Todo"

HONORABLE MENTION FOR POETRY

Walter McDonald
"The Barn Five Miles from Town"

Here's to your continued success!!!

The winning manuscripts are featured in Volume II, No. 3.

The
BLOOMSBURY
REVIEW
A BOOK MAGAZINE

SIMPLY THE BEST!
BOOK REVIEWS • INTERVIEWS • ESSAYS
POETRY • PROFILES

For more than 15 years, we've been reviewing some of the best books from presses small and large, interviewing some of the most fascinating writers you are likely to meet, and publishing poetry, profiles, and essays. Tony Hillerman said we were "the best book magazine in America." Alex Blackburn called us "the best critical review of books in the United States." (But don't worry, we don't let it go to our heads.) Clarissa Pinkola Estés called us the "best rag in the nation" (but we don't hold it against her.)

One year: $16.00 • Two years: $28.00 • Three years: $36.00
Ask for *The Bloomsbury Review* at your local bookstore, or contact:

The Bloomsbury Review
1762 Emerson Street
Denver, CO 80218
303/863-0406; FAX: 303/863-0408

Order Form

One–year subscriptions are $18 ($15 for students and teachers). Sample copies are $6.50. Gift subscriptions make a perfect gift at a special rate of $14. The first issue of gift subscriptions will be sent with a card in your name. Add $15.00 per one-year subscription for subscriptions outside of North America. If you are not completely satisfied, we will promptly send you a refund.

Subscriber's name _____

Street/Apt. No. _____

City/State/Zip _____

Phone _____

* GIFT SUBSCRIPTION:

Recipient's name _____

Street/Apt. No. _____

City/State/Zip _____

Sender's name/address/phone _____

* GIFT SUBSCRIPTION:

Recipient's name _____

Street/Apt. No. _____

City/State/Zip _____

Sender's name/address/phone _____

Please begin my subscription with the next issue (Vol. III, No. 2).

****

Many Mountains Moving is now on the Web.
We invite you to come visit our site at:

http://www.concentric.net/~mmminc

We love to hear feedback from our readers.
Please feel free to e-mail us at mmminc@concentric.net.

Send check or money order to:
Many Mountains Moving, 420 22nd St., Boulder, CO 80302 U.S.A.

Phone (303)545-9942; Fax (303)444-6510

[ ] Yes, I would also like to order previous issues of
Many Mountains Moving for only $6.50 each:
__Inaugural Issue __Vol. I, No. 2 __Vol. I, No. 3
__Vol. II, No. 1   SOLD OUT Vol. II, No. 2   __Vol. II, No. 3

[ ] Yes, I would like to order five issues of the first two volumes
of Many Mountains Moving
(excepting Volume II, No. 2, which is sold out)
for only $30

Amount Enclosed: $__

The inaugural issue of Many Mountains Moving features work by Robert Bly, Lorna Dee Cervantes, Diane Glancy, Jonathan Holden, Walter McDonald, Peter Meinke, Naomi Shihab Nye, Alicia Ostriker, Marge Piercy, Virgil Suarez, Luis Alberto Urrea and Diane Wakoski and many more.

Volume I, No. 2 features work by Sherman Alexie, Patricia Ammann, Tony Ardizzone, Susan Casey, Debra Kang Dean, Jonathan Holden, Lawson Fusao Inada, Bruce Jacobs, Lyn Lifshin, Alicia Ostriker, Adrienne Rich, Ralph Salisbury, David Sims, Mary McLaughlin Slechta, Karen Swenson, Ingrid Wendt, Carlos Kareem Windham, and Monica Wood.

Volume I, No. 3 has a special section celebrating Indian poets. This issue features work by Patricia Ammann, Paramita Banerjee, Christopher Bank, Ricia Anne Chansky, Helena Christensen, Susan Clements, Enid Dame, Buddahadeb Dasgupta, Manjush Dasgupta, Jyotirmoy Datta, Michael Dorsey, Allen Ginsberg, Gary Holthaus, Arun Kolatkar, Alex Kuo, Anuradha Mahapatra, Lynne McMahon, Peter Michelson, Ayyappa Paniker, Savithri Rajeevan, Subodh Sarkar, K. Satchidanandan, Mallika Sengupta, Menak Shivdasani, Barry Silesky, Kristine Somerville, W.D. Wetherell, Kathryn Winograd, and Carolyn Wright.

Volume II, No. 1 is a special issue on "Burning Issues," guest edited by Luis Alberto Urrea. Contributors include Kim Addonizio, Rane Arroyo, Amiri Baraka, Laure-Anne Bosselaar, Kurt Brown, Carolyn Campbell, May-lee Chai, Leonard Chang, Charen, Allison deFreese, Ellen Dudley, Susan Eisenberg, Michelle Esmailian, David Fedo, Annie Finch, Carol Frost, Sonia Gomez, Jean Heilprin, Lawson Fusao Inada, M.J. Iuppa, Lysa James, Allison Joseph, Richard Krawiec, Lyn Lifshin, Esteban Martinez, Nancy McCleery, Gregory McNamee, Tara Menon, Ed Ochester, Allan Peterson, Swami Anand Prahlad, Michael Ramos, Juliet Rodeman, Sangeeta Reddy, Terry Lee Schifferns, Alison Stone, Jeff Thomson, Boyd White, Manual Vélez, Judith Vollmer, Terry Wolverton, and Renate Wood.

Volume II, No. 2 is sold out.

Volume II, No.3 features Deborah Batterman, Amanda Castro, Leonard Chang, Eddie Chuculate, Jack Collom, Mary Crow, Enid Dame, Susan Eisenberg, Joel Ensana, Kay Hawkins, Mark Irwin, Luke July, Ariana-Sophia Kartsonis, Miodrag Kojadinoi´c, Yusef Komunyakaa, Daniela Kuper, Walter McDonald, Gregory McNamee, Lani Kwan Meilgaard, Kent Meyers, Netzahualcoyotl, Alissa Reardon Norton, Naomi Shihab Nye, Olga Orozco, Wang Ping, Michael Ramos, T. Maurice Savoie, Julie Shigekuni, Michele Spring-Moore, David Swerdlow, Carol Turner, Diane Wakoski, Ken Waldman, Boyd White, Gary Whitehead, Sarah Wolbach, Terry Wolverton, Lisa Horton Zimmerman.

In upcoming issues...

AWP Intro Award manuscripts

Laurel Blossom

Nora Booth

Special issue guest-edited by
Laure-Anne Bosselaar and Kurt Brown

Cayle

Debra Kang Dean

S.K. Duff

Alice Fogel

Lucia Getsi

Ignacio Gómez-Palacio

Sam Hamill

Staci Leigh Haynes

Lawson Fusao Inada

Mark Irwin

George Kalamaras

Ursula K. Le Guin

Carol Mahler

Interview with Speer Morgan,
author of *The Whipping Boy*

Kellie Paluck

Mary Byrne Park

Barry Silesky

Katherine Smith

Ken Waldman

Ronald Wallace

Julia Wendell

Martha Wiseman